A King Production presents...

MAFIA Princess

The Takeover

PART 5

A NOVEL

JOY DEJA KING

AND CHRIS BOOKER

CH

ISBN 13: 978-0991389001
ISBN 10: 099138900X
Cover concept by Joy Deja King
Cover layout and graphic design by www.MarionDesigns.com
Typesetting: Keith Saunders

Library of Congress Cataloging-in-Publication Data;
A King Production
Mafia Princess Part 4 by: Joy Deja King/Chris Booker
For complete Library of Congress Copyright info visit;
www.joydejaking.com
Twitter @joydejaking

A King Production
P.O. Box 912, Collierville, TN 38027

A King Production and the above portrayal log are trademarks of
A King Production LLC

Dedication

This Book is Dedicated to My:
Family, Readers and Supporters.
I LOVE you guys so much. Please believe that!!

—Joy Deja King

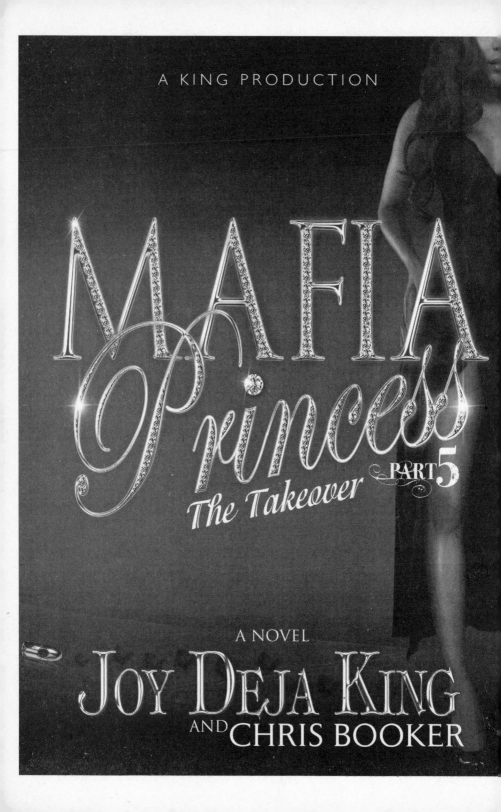

A KING PRODUCTION

MAFIA
Princess
The Takeover

PART 5

A NOVEL

JOY DEJA KING
AND CHRIS BOOKER

Prologue

"I should've known," Semaj said, walking into the empty ballroom where the Tent meeting was about to take place.

She looked out the door that led to the lobby and saw people rushing for the front entrance. The sounds of women screaming and men yelling for someone to call 911 let Semaj know that the bodies in the elevator were found. All the chaos prompted the other members to get up and leave, they didn't want to be around when the police showed up.

"Yo ma, we gotta get out of here," Qua insisted, grabbing Semaj by the arm.

"Hold up. Dis bitch is tryna kill me and I gotta end dis shit before she become successful the next go 'round," Semaj said, standing at the threshold of the door.

"Yeah, I know, but we can't do shit right now but get da hell up out of here before the cops come,"

Qua shot back, looking out into the lobby.

When Semaj went into deep thought, it didn't matter where she was at, she just froze. She didn't want to blow her chances of exposing Nikolai, and she definitely didn't want to give her the opportunity to retreat back to her homeland. Although she wasn't the boss over in Russia, she was well-connected and loved by just about everybody. Even if the members from the 16 Tent wanted her killed, if she made it back home, her people wouldn't give her up. Semaj knew that and wanted to avoid it.

"They can't leave," Semaj said, snapping out of her deep thoughts.

She looked out into the lobby and saw a couple of police officers walking up to the desk. She stepped back into the ballroom, pulling her gun from her back pocket. Qua closed the door and looked at Semaj with curiosity, wondering what she planned on doing with the gun. He had already forgotten all about her last comment.

"If Nikolai leaves now, we'll probably never see her again," Semaj said, cuffing the gun in her shirt.

She began wiping her fingerprints off the gun. Then, when she felt like she was done, she stuffed it down into one of the flowerpots against the wall. Qua did the same thing before they both left the ballroom.

"How do you plan on keeping Nikolai here? She and every other Tent member have their own private jet. She can leave whenever she want to and that's if she hadn't already bounced by now," Qua reasoned as they walked towards the lobby.

The elevators were in the lobby area, and so as they walked by, Semaj looked over and saw Raul and Julio's bodies lying there. Several police officers were on the scene, already taping it off.

Once outside, Semaj stopped, turned around, and faced Qua. "We gone have to do it by force," she said, answering his previous question.

"By force, are you serious?" he asked, making sure he heard her correctly.

Holding Nikolai hostage was almost equivalent to putting a bullet in her head. The 16 Tent had strict rules against actions like this and none of the members were exempt from the punishment behind not having a valid reason for the action.

"You know that if you do this—"

"Yeah, I know," she said cutting him off.

Semaj was well aware that if she went through with this, she didn't have any other choice, but to bring forth the proof of Nikolai's attempted assassination. If she couldn't do it, the rest of the Tent members would kill her as a result of her actions. Death seemed a little harsh as the punishment, but these rules and regulations were put in place for a reason.

Semaj understood that and was willing to put her life on the line in order to bring forth the truth. It wasn't like she had much of a choice anyways. If she didn't get her out of the way soon, Nikolai was gonna end up killing her anyhow. So, at this point, she really didn't have anything to lose.

Chapter 1

"Ron, my man," Agent Davis greeted, as he and his partner, Agent King, jumped out of the all black Crown Victoria.

"Aww shit," Ron gasped, throwing his head back.

Ron had a couple of his boys out there and the last thing he needed was for Davis to expose him. Davis played it cool though, pretending that he was only there to break his balls. He grabbed Ron and slung him up against the car while Agent King put the other two men up against the wall.

"Do you really think I won't put yo' black ass in jail," Davis said, in a low tone so that only Ron could hear him. "Or better yet, how about I tell yo' boys that you out here working for me," Davis threatened, as he continued to pat him down.

Davis was getting fed up with Ron's half-assed info, and not producing anything he'd promised. The DEA was thirsty for blood and they wanted

Sosa bad. Up until Davis met Ron, Sosa had been like a ghost to the bureau. They knew that Sosa existed and that he or she was a major player in the drug trafficking market in New York, but they could never get close enough. Ron had become their hope.

"Call my phone in 'bout two hours," Ron mumbled.

"Bullshit," Davis shot back, turning him around to face him. "Give me one good reason why I shouldn't take you with me right now," Davis said.

"Two hours," was all Ron could say without drawing any more attention to himself.

Davis looked at him and saw the pleas pouring out of his eyes. He knew that this time, Ron might have something good for him. Davis really couldn't afford to pass on a possible lead, but if Ron didn't have something substantial to work with he was going to jail and Davis wasn't going to second-guess it.

"Two hours," Davis mumbled, before pushing Ron off of his car.

Ron backed up with his hands in the air and watched as Davis and King got back into their car and pulled off.

"Yo, who da fuck was dat?" one of Ron's boys said, fixing his clothes from King's vicious shakedown.

"I don't know my nigga, but I'm about to get

out of here," Ron responded, heading for his car.

He was leaving but not for the reasons his boys thought he was. Ron was trying to avoid prison, and if he didn't come up with something good within the next two hours, prison was exactly where he was going.

"*Hola, mama,*" Vikingo greeted when he cracked his eyes open and saw Semaj sitting in a chair next to his bed.

Vikingo's condition was still critical, but he was stable. A couple of more surgeries were necessary, but only to remove the few bullet fragments he had left in him. His permanent injuries were another story, one that Semaj didn't want to bring up at the moment.

"Hi, handsome." She smiled, bringing his hand up to her lips and kissing it. "You been asleep too long," Semaj said, getting up from her chair, leaning over, and pressing her lips on his forehead. "The doctor said that you're going to be alright..."

Vikingo chuckled through his pain. "You know Semaj, this is the first time you ever lied to me," he responded.

Semaj put her head down. She felt ashamed and didn't want to be the one who told him the truth.

"I guess that's why I can't feel my legs," Vikingo said, looking up at her.

Semaj didn't know what to say. She tried to think of some words to comfort him but she couldn't come up with any. How do you tell your fiancé that he will never be able to walk again, nor will he ever be able to have sexual intercourse with his wife? There was no easy way to say those words, nor any way to comfort him for that matter.

"So I'm guessing the wedding is off..."

"Shhhhh! Don't talk like that. You know I love you, Vikingo, and the wedding is still on. I don't care if I gotta wheel you down the aisle myself," Semaj assured, rubbing her hand gently through his hair.

It sounded good rolling off her tongue, but the truth of the matter was that Semaj didn't know what she was going to do. Being around Qua these past few weeks had her torn. Her mind was telling her to be honorable and stand by Vikingo, but her heart was screaming for her to be with Qua.

"What's wrong?" he asked, "And don't say nothing because I can see it in your eyes that something is wrong," Vikingo whispered through his dry mouth.

Semaj did have a lot on her mind. Besides the love triangle she was fighting, her life was in complete chaos. With the condition Vikingo was in, she didn't want to bother him with the details, especially since he wasn't in the position to help.

"Go ahead. Spit it out," Vikingo insisted.

Although he wasn't able to protect her physically, he still felt that Semaj was his responsibility.

Semaj didn't know where to start. Vikingo had missed so much being in a coma. The last thing he remembered was the poachers stealing from the warehouse and him being shot in the process of trying to stop them. He was clueless to the fact that somebody from the 16 Tent was trying to kill her, and at one point they were almost successful in doing so. Vikingo didn't know that Semaj was forced to turn up and show her dominance throughout Colombia, killing any and everybody who posed a threat to her and her family. Vikingo also didn't know about Sosa being kidnapped and tortured in the jungle by Raul's people, and he definitely didn't know that Qua was back in the picture, holding Semaj down and riding with her every move. Vikingo didn't know any of this, but Semaj was about to tell him, that is, everything except the part about Qua.

Ron looked down at his phone when it started ringing. He knew that from the blocked number it had to be Agent Davis calling to see what he had. He was right on point too, exactly two hours from the time they pulled up on Ron and his boys sitting on the corner.

Ron sat in his car and looked out of the

window, debating on whether or not to answer it. It was a struggle he had within himself. He hated the position that he was in because at the end of the day he was going to hurt a lot of people, mainly his right hand man, Qua, who was about to get caught up in the mix.

"Yo, what up," Ron answered his phone, rubbing his forehead in a stressful manner.

"I hope you got something good for me," Agent Davis said, looking out into the streets as he drove down Broadway.

"Yeah, meet me at 47th and 3rd Avenue tomorrow at 12 noon. Sosa should be delivering 200 kilos to my boy. Just make sure he don't go to jail," Ron said then hung up the phone.

He was disgusted with himself for what he was doing, but at the same time he didn't want to spend the rest of his life in prison. Agent Davis held the keys to his fate and he hated that even more.

Qua leaned up against the convertible beamer waiting for Semaj to emerge from the hospital after being inside for a couple of hours. Instead of going inside with her like he started to, Qua decided to give her some space and time alone with Vikingo. He wasn't really feeling it, but the fact still remained that Vikingo was her fiancé and they were due to be married sometime in the near future. He didn't like it, but he had to respect it.

"You good, ma?" Qua asked Semaj as she walked up to the car.

She just looked at him and nodded her head in the affirmative. He could tell that she was lying. From their long history of being with each other, Qua could always get a good read on Semaj.

"Come 'er," Qua said, opening his arms so that he could hug her. "Tell Q about it," he spoke softly.

Walking into his arms seemed like the natural thing to do, and she did it, resting her body up against his and leaning her head against his chest. When he wrapped his arms around her and held her tight, Semaj felt safe and secure, something she hadn't felt since Vikingo had been in the hospital.

"I wanna tell you something, but I need it to stay between us for now," Semaj began. "A'ight?" she asked, looking up at him for his confirmation.

"Maj, you know you don't even have to say that. Everything we talk about is between me and you," Qua responded, looking her in the eyes.

"Qua, my feelings run deep for you. In fact, I think I'm still in love with you," Semaj admitted.

"And what's wrong with that?" Qua shot back.

Just like a man, Qua wasn't thinking about nobody else's heart, but his. If he had it his way, him and Semaj would ride off into the sunset together and live happily ever after. Semaj probably was the only one thinking about Vikingo.

"I'm suppose to be gettin' married in less than a month and here I am in love with someone else."

"Well maybe you're getting married to the wrong man," Qua stated with all honesty. "You and I both know that we suppose to be together, Maj. Our connection is way too deep to ignore and you know it."

Semaj hated to admit it, but what he said about the connection was true. It seemed like whenever Semaj got around Qua, nothing else mattered. He conjured up feelings that were unexplainable. Semaj could only surmise that Qua was her soul mate.

"Oh shit," Semaj said, looking down at her watch. "Your shipment suppose to be coming into the city in a few hours. I have to take care of some things before it gets here," she said, backing out of his grasp and heading around to the passenger side of the car.

"So what you wanna do about the other situation?" Qua asked, referring to Nikolai.

"I still got a business to run. Trust me, she's not going anywhere," Semaj told him, opening the passenger side door. "Besides, I know you need some work. This city is dry as hell." She giggled, getting into the car.

Qua smiled as he got into the car, too. But in

all actuality, the city was dry right now due to Sosa being out of the picture. He couldn't afford to take his people through a drought right now. It could mean losing valuable clientele, and for Qua that was unacceptable.

Chapter 2

"You think this guy pulling our chain?" Agent Davis looked over and asked Agent King.

"I don't know, but nothing beats a blank right now," King answered before biting down on his hot, roast beef sandwich.

"Hell, do you know how many stripes we'll get if we take down Sosa, the legend?" Davis said, looking out the driver side window at the few pedestrians walking by.

Not only would a bust like this earn them stripes it would surely move Davis and King up the ranks. Ever since Sosa's name began ringing in the streets, no cop, no detective, and no federal agent could get close enough to the ghost. The people knew that the person behind the name existed, and that whoever it was flooded the streets of New York with cocaine, they just didn't have the face to go with the name.

"I tell you one thing, if Ron don't come

through for us this time, he's going to jail today," Davis said, turning around to look at the bag of evidence he had on Ron sitting in the back seat.

King chuckled at him before taking another bite of his sandwich. He found it funny that Davis actually held on to the .45 Ruger, three kilos of cocaine and the 27 ounces of crack. In the eyes of the court that evidence would be considered tainted, seeing how Davis had been riding around with it for weeks without checking it in. Ron didn't know that, though. It scared the hell out of him every time he saw it and thought about the life sentence it carried.

Qua sat inside of My Kidz Pizzeria off 47th and 3rd Avenue, eating a slice of cheese pizza by the window. He was waiting for Ron to show up so that he could take the new shipment to the stash house. Once there, the product would be cut up and broken down for street retail. The hood was in desperate need of it, too.

"Where da fuck is dis nigga at?" Qua mumbled to himself, as he looked out the large picture window.

A few minutes later, Ron's Range Rover pulled up and he parked right across the street from the pizzeria. Qua watched as he hopped out, dusted his clothes off then slammed the door before walking across the street. Qua still couldn't put his finger on it, but there was something about Ron that was different.

Qua had been analyzing him over the past few days and had noticed a change in Ron's attitude. He was quieter as opposed to being loud and cocky like he normally would be; and instead of being sober and on point, he was always high and slipping.

"What up my nigga," Ron greeted, walking over to the table where Qua was sitting and giving him dap.

"Yo son, what's good wit' you," Qua spit back, taking another bite of his pizza.

"You know, same shit different toilet. I see ol' girl finally came through. It's right on time cause we ain't got shit," Ron said, waving to the waitress to come over.

One thing about Qua is that he really wasn't the type to bite his tongue, nor did he let shit bottle up inside of him until it exploded. If he had something to say, it was going to get said, and it didn't matter who he was talking to.

"Yo my nigga. You been actin' funny lately. What's really good wit' you?" Qua questioned, looking at Ron with a straight face.

The same dumb look Ron had for the past week or so came right over his face. It was a sneaky look with a hint of paranoia. Ron tried to clean it up as much as he could without giving Qua too much to work with.

"My nigga, I'm just goin' through some shit right now," Ron said in a low tone as the waitress walked up and put his slice of pizza on the table.

For Qua, that wasn't enough. He needed to know more. Qua sat there and waited for the waitress to walk off before he pried further.

"So what, I'm not yo' boy now. You don't trust me wit' yo' business?" Qua said.

Qua's sharp looks and raw questions were beginning to cut through Ron's armor with ease. He had to come up with something before Qua eventually put two and two together. If he did that and found out Ron was working for the police, their friendship would be deadened, and Qua wouldn't hesitate putting a bullet in his head for his act of disloyalty.

"Yo, my mom got cancer, B," Ron lied. "She had it for a minute, too, and now she talkin' crazy like she don't wanna go through chemo," he said, putting the saddest look he could come up with on his face.

His lie was convincing because Qua ate it all up. He felt bad, getting up from his seat and giving Ron a thug hug. It was a little extreme, but that was the best Ron could come up with on such short notice.

"You know what my nigga, we gon' take care of this business and put this work back out on the streets, then after that, we'll sit down and try to figure out a way to get Ms. Wahita to take the chemo," Qua said, patting Ron on his back.

"A'ight my nigga. Dat sound like a plan," Ron responded, nodding his head.

Ron sat there and finished his slice of pizza while Qua jumped on the phone to check on the shipment. He was nervous as hell, but at this point, Ron wasn't in a position to be turning back. He was wired for sound and Agent Davis along with Agent Mason were sitting in the wing praying this was their big chance to take down the infamous Sosa.

Semaj took care of the business she needed to in order to assure that the two tons of cocaine made it safely to the states. Not only that, but she also had to make sure Qua's shipment got to him on time as well. Since Sosa was still recovering from the whole jungle ordeal, Semaj had to pick up the slack and serve everybody in the cities of New York, New Jersey, and Philadelphia. That even included Qua, whom she decided to serve personally.

"Turn down 47th and go to the warehouses at the end of the street," Semaj directed her driver.

Her caravan consisted of three black Chevy Tahoes with tinted windows, four men per truck—all which were heavily armed. Even though Qua was the first person she was meeting up with, her guards still had the green light to shoot anything moving funny. It was too much money and too much cocaine involved to be playing games. Not that she felt Qua would do anything crazy, she just knew how the game could go.

"Heads up! We got three black Tahoes coming down 47th," Davis said, looking through his binoculars. Mason sat in the passenger side trying to adjust the listening device that was sitting on his lap. The conversation coming through his headphones had a lot of static, but Mason was able to make out Ron's voice.

"They're slowing down," Davis said, looking attentively.

Until they knew for sure it was Sosa, they didn't want to have a thousand agents and U.S. Marshalls sitting around waiting. If need be and necessary, they were only a phone call and about seven minutes away. It was nothing to push the button about.

"Can you hear them?" Davis asked, lowering the binoculars.

"It's getting clearer. Just give me a second," Mason answered.

He did a little more tweaking on the box and after about 45 seconds, Mason could hear both Ron and Qua loud and clear. Davis snapped a couple of pictures, too.

"We got action," Mason said, taking the headphones off so that Davis could hear, too.

"Whoa, whoa, whoa, look at this," Davis said, putting the binoculars back up to his eyes.

All four doors swung open to the first Tahoe and out jumped four men, heavily armed with submachine guns. Davis could tell by the way they were dressed, Ron and Qua had to be dealing with somebody important. Regular cats on the streets didn't wear suits to drug buys. It definitely looked like the work of a boss.

"You think that's..." Mason began.

"Nah, these guys are security. They're only checking out the area," Davis responded.

He was right too, because two of the men looked up and down the street while another looked up at the warehouse. The last of the four men circled around Qua's car, looking inside for anything suspicious.

"Yo son, these muthafuckas don't play no games," Ron said, watching the tall, long-haired Colombian walking around the car. "I didn't know Sosa ride so hard," he said.

"That's cause this ain't Sosa, my nigga," Qua shot back with a serious face. "Now stop talking and stop moving before you get us both shot."

Qua knew that Semaj's men were trained to shoot first and fuck asking questions. They were there to protect her, and would do so by any means necessary.

After about a minute the whole area was secured and the four men walked back to the truck, but did not get in. One of them got on the phone for about two seconds and then moments later, the back passenger side door of the last Tahoe opened up and Semaj jumped out, looking bossy as ever. She had on a black leather skirt, white fitted silk blouse, and a pair of Hollywood glam sunglasses. On her feet was a pair of black Giuseppe's.

Qua and Ron got out of the car together. The guards were about to walk over and pat them down, but Semaj waved them off. Qua looked at her and couldn't help but smile. Just hours ago she didn't look anything like this.

"Protocol," Semaj said, walking up to Qua and Ron.

As soon as she got within a few feet of Ron, her pager began vibrating inside of her jacket. She jumped from it, not expecting for it to go off. She looked at Qua, then cut her eyes over at Ron. Qua could see the change in her demeanor and wondered what was wrong.

"So, are we gonna do business or what?" Ron asked, breaking the silence.

Semaj cut her eyes back over to Qua and smiled. She shook her head and began to back up towards her men. Qua raised his hands in a confused manner trying to figure out what was going on.

"I'll call you later!" Semaj yelled out before walking off and jumping back into the truck.

Qua stood there stuck, watching as the three trucks sped off down the street. He looked over at Ron, who had shrugged his shoulders, confused himself about what just went down. All Qua could do was get back into his car and leave as well, hoping that Semaj would call soon to let him know what was going on. Whatever it was, something wasn't right.

Chapter 3

When Sosa stepped off the G-4 private jet, she was surprised to see Santos standing there leaning up against a dark green Benz. She was expecting for it to be Semaj picking her up, but it meant a lot for it to be him. If it weren't for Santos being on parole, he would have flown to Colombia to pick Sosa up himself.

"You gon' stand there looking handsome or are you going to help me down these steps," Sosa said, pointing her cane at him.

Her leg was still messed up from the AK-47 bullet that ripped through it, but she was fortunate enough to keep her leg. Believe it or not, the doctor who used the medicines he abstracted from the jungle plants saved Sosa from having to have her leg amputated. Whatever he gave her, fought off infections and preserved tissue, muscles, and a healthy blood count.

Santos walked up the short flight of steps and

stood right in front of her. He missed the hell out of her and was so happy to see Sosa, especially alive.

"You know I'm not gonna let you leave this country again," he said, lifting her chin up to kiss her.

"I don't think you gotta worry about that," Sosa assured, thinking about the whole ordeal she'd been through in the jungle.

Santos scooped her off of her feet and carried her down the steps and to the car. Though he wanted to take her straight home and keep her under his guardianship, Semaj gave him strict orders to bring Sosa to her. That was the only way Semaj would agree to let him pick Sosa up by himself. There were a few important people that needed to see her, and she still had to explain to the Tent families what happened to her. Not that she had to explain the entire situation, but it was imperative to let the other families know how foul Raul was.

Semaj hung up the phone after speaking with the last of the Tent families, informing them not to leave the city because another meeting was taking place. She looked out of the tall panorama window in Murda Mitch's condo in deep thought. She hadn't seen Qua since yesterday and was anxious to talk to him. There were a couple of questions that needed to be asked to determine whether or not their friendship would last.

"How's daddy's princess?" Mitch said, walking up to Semaj at the window and kissing the side of her cheek.

"I'm good, Daddy," she said in a non-convincing voice.

"Now you know you can't lie to save ya life," he joked. "You don't think I know when something is wrong with my daughter?" he said, standing in front of the glass to block her view.

A knock at the door caught both of their attention. Semaj had an idea who it was because she had invited Qua over to get some things straightened out.

"Come in!" Mitch yelled out, not worried about who it was on the other side of the door.

Mitch thought his condo was the most secure place in NYC right now. Anytime he stayed there he had armed men in the lobby, one outside his door and two more inside the condo with him. Not to mention the fact that he himself walked around the condo armed.

When the front door opened, Qua had just finished getting patted down by the guard. He entered the condo and looked around, noticing two other guards that got up from their seats and stood to the side. Qua could feel that the welcome wasn't warm and it made him very uneasy and irritated.

"Qua, don't mind the security. I can never

be too safe wit' my princess around," Murda Mitch said, walking over and giving Qua a handshake.

"Yeah, you might wanna tighten up on that security thing," Qua responded, shoving his hand into his pants.

He fiddled around in his pants before pulling out a black compact .45 automatic. The two guards reached for their guns, but Murda Mitch stopped them.

"Y'all two would have been shot," Qua told the two guards before placing the gun back on his hip where it was originally.

Mitch smiled then threw his arm around Qua's neck, leading him over to Semaj. Mitch couldn't hide how pissed he was about Qua exposing how lackluster his highly paid security team was.

"I'll leave you two alone. I got some shit to handle," Mitch said, walking off and leaving Qua and Semaj standing by the window so that he could chastise his guards.

It was a little quiet for a second before Qua broke the silence. "Maj, what's goin' on? And why do I feel all this negative energy coming from you. I mean, yesterday at the drop point you backed out and drove off without sayin' anything, and then you wouldn't answer my calls."

Semaj didn't say anything at first. She wanted to see if her pager was going to go off before she spoke, but it didn't. Semaj was ready to skip the bullshit and get straight to the serious matter at hand. She could only ask Qua what she needed to know in one way; raw and uncut, and it didn't matter if he liked it or not.

"Are you workin' for the police?" Semaj asked with a straight face.

When it came to her freedom and the freedom of her family, Semaj didn't have any picks. Unfortunately for Qua, he took it as though she had disrespected him to the utmost. He looked at her like she was crazy and felt the urge to punch Semaj in her mouth, but instead he just laughed it off to keep from snapping.

"Semaj, did you just call me a rat?" Qua asked, raising his eyebrow.

"Qua, it ain't like that. I just—"

"You got me fucked up, Maj, and for you to even ask me some dumb shit like that let's me know exactly how you think of me," Qua stated with venom in his voice.

Qua's anger quickly turned into hurt and Semaj could see that she may have crossed the line. By the pain in his eyes, she already had the answer to her question.

"I'm out, yo," Qua said, bumping Semaj as he passed by her.

"Qua, hold up for a second," Semaj pleaded, grabbing the back of his shirt. "I got this thing while I was in Colombia," she said, pulling out the pager looking device. "If anything like wires, bugs, or tracking devices come within five feet of it and it vibrates. Yesterday, when I walked up on you and yo' boy it went off. That guy you was with had on a wire," Semaj said, trying to clean up the fact that she questioned him about it first.

Qua grabbed the little black box from Semaj to examine it. At the same time, Semaj snapped her fingers at one of the guards to go and retrieve something from out one of the bedrooms. Qua looked at the pager then back up at Semaj. He was still hurt and angry, but his focus now shifted over to Ron. His gut told him that something wasn't right with Ron, but never in a million years did he think his boy would be working for the police. He still didn't believe it, and until he found out for himself, Qua wasn't going to put that kind of mark on him.

"Yo, let me get out of here. I'ma take this with me," he said, tucking the pager in his pocket.

"Wait, take this wit' you," she said, looking over at the guard bringing two large duffle bags out of the room.

It was the 200-kilo shipment he was supposed to get yesterday, but Qua really wasn't feeling Semaj right now. "Nah ma, I'm good. You hold on to that," he said, then turned around and walked out of the condo.

Nikolai sat in the back seat while her driver pulled into the airport. They drove into the hanger where Marco's private jet was waiting. Marco had opted to stay in New York for the next meeting, but allowed Nikolai to use his jet since she flew into the city with him.

"I want to be in the air in ten minutes," Nikolai told the pilot as she exited the car.

The pilot stood there with a frightened look on his face, not responding to Nikolai's demand. As she walked towards the jet, the pilot remained there, frozen like an icicle. Nikolai got to the jet and turned around seeing that the pilot didn't move.

"Let's go, let's go," she said, snapping her fingers at him.

The pilot still didn't move. That's when Nikolai saw it. Two black Chrysler 300s pulled into the hanger, stopping right in front of the jet. Nikolai had two guards with her, but even they weren't stupid enough to draw their weapons after seeing several men hopping out one of the cars and carrying large assault rifles. Neither of the armed men said anything but rather stood there with their fingers on the outer part of the trigger.

"Who are you and why are you blocking my plane?" Nikolai yelled out from the bottom of the stairs that went up to the door of the jet.

Nobody answered her, but then the back door to the second Chrysler opened up. Murda Mitch got out of the car dressed in all black. He walked up to Nikolai in a cool, calm,1 and casual manner, not phased at all by the two guards standing in front of her.

"Nikolai, my daughter had a feeling that you would try and leave," Mitch said, placing his hands in his pants pocket. "It's unfortunate, but I'm gonna have to ask you to come with me."

"Come with you? I'm not going anywhere with you," Nikolai said defiantly. "You'll have to kill me right here, right now," she shouted.

"Well that's optional, too," Mitch responded, looking over his shoulder at his gunmen who were more than willing to open fire on her and her men. "Look Nikolai, you can save the tough act. You and I both know you don't wanna die at the hands of these young, black, African-American men from the ghetto," Mitch said.

Who Mitch had with him was a bunch of hood niggas he rounded up from his old neighborhood. They were grimy, gutta, and fresh out of Brooklyn. They even dressed hood, wearing jeans, t-shirts, and Timberland boots.

Nikolai knew that Mitch couldn't kill her, especially being a member of the Tent, but at the same time, she didn't want to take any chances with her life. In her mind, she felt like she was too good to die at the hands of 'a nobody'. Plus, it looked like her death would be painful had they started shooting.

"Go and let Marco know what's happening," Nikolai said, leaning over one of her guards.

She walked past her men and headed for the Chrysler, only to be stopped at the back door and patted down thoroughly. When it was determined that she was unarmed, the back door opened for her. Mitch got into the back seat with her, not to converse, but to keep his eyes on Nikolai until they got to where they were going.

Santos pulled up to the coffee shop where Semaj told him to bring Sosa after they spent some time together. Of course he had to call before they showed up, which he did. Sosa was already on point and knew that more than likely Semaj was having a surprise party of some sort.

"I hate surprise parties," Sosa looked over and told Santos with a smile on her face.

"Who said anything about a surprise party?" He chuckled.

Sosa looked over at the coffee shop, noticing all the blinds were closed and not one customer entered or exited. The luxury vehicles parked throughout the block was also a dead giveaway. Santos glanced out the window, noticing all the cars, too, and just shook his head.

"Just try to act like you're surprised," he said, leaning over and kissing her.

Sosa just smiled getting out of the car. She had a little limp, but was able to walk on her own without the assistance of the cane. Santos was by her side anyway, just in case she needed to lean up against him for some support.

As soon as they got up to the front door of the coffee shop, it swung open and none other than Semaj was standing there with a huge smile on her face. There was a crowd of people behind her, but Sosa really didn't get a chance to see them because Semaj closed the door behind her so they could have some privacy before everybody else rushed her.

The moment Semaj wrapped her arms around Sosa she began to cry. Back in Colombia, crying could be a sign of weakness, but here in New York it could be a sign of love. That's all Semaj had for her cousin— love—and she was so happy to see her alive and well considering everything she'd been through.

"I'm... I'm sorry. I didn't..." Semaj tried to talk through her tears.

The last time she had seen Sosa was when they were in the jungle and several armed men surrounded her with AK-47 rifles, while Semaj and her caravan drove away. Having to leave Sosa in that jungle was by far the hardest thing Semaj ever had to do in her life, and a part of her always felt horrible for doing it.

"Girl, would you stop. You got me all teary-eyed." Sosa chuckled, patting Semaj on her back as they hugged.

Semaj didn't want to let her go, but she knew she had to before the people inside got antsy and came outside. They both took a few extra seconds wiping their faces dry before heading inside of the coffee shop where just about everyone who knew Sosa personally, was waiting.

Not all, but even a couple of members from the 16 Tent were there to welcome Sosa home. A lot of people were happy for her return, especially Sosa's number one fan.

"Mommy, Mommy," Nyala yelled, pushing her way through the crowd.

Sosa swooped down and grabbed her up, hugging and holding her daughter tightly. She had to have kissed Nyala fifty times all over. It was as if the pain in Sosa's leg immediately vanished because she twirled, squatted, and bounced up and down with Nyala without limping the least bit. This was the highlight of her return and nothing or nobody else in the room even mattered.

Chapter 4

Agent Davis sat at his cubicle staring at a picture of Semaj that he took at the drop site. Ron was missing in action again, so Davis was unable to get any clarity on who she was. From the looks of the heavy security around her, Davis knew she was someone of importance. The only reason why he didn't move on her at the drop was because there wasn't a transaction of any money or drugs to make an arrest.

"Did you try to call Ron?" Agent Mason asked walking up behind Davis's chair.

"Yeah. His phone goes straight to voicemail. You feel like taking a ride?" Davis questioned, sticking Semaj's picture up on his computer screen.

Ron wasn't that hard to find. The day that they took Ron's car to the impound lot to search it; they put a GPS tracker by the engine. In case Ron decided to use his Range Rover to get around, Davis put a GPS tracker on it as well, all without a warrant.

"Are you guys aware of the double homicide at the Four Seasons last week?" another agent walked up and asked both Davis and Mason.

"Yeah, I heard. NYC homicide division is on it," Davis responded, getting up from his chair.

It was common for federal agents to share information on crimes going on in the city. Sometimes certain crimes trigger federal penalties or could be on an extension to an ongoing federal investigation. Only being a double homicide wasn't really enough to grab Davis's attention, that is, until the other agent continued to speak.

"Well did you know... Hey, that's Semaj Richardson," the agent said, changing the topic when he saw Semaj's picture on Davis's computer screen.

"Who?" Agent Mason asked with a curious look on his face.

"Semaj Richardson. She's connected to the Milano family. I'm not sure what role she plays but when we were investigating the Milanos a couple of years back, we identified her as possibly being the head of the family once Gio Milano was assassinated," Agent Flint explained.

"So what happened to the investigation?" Davis asked.

"Our investigation went cold after most of the Milano family was murdered. Semaj over there," he

---

pointed to her picture, "was like the last of them. She disappeared a while back. Rumor has it she moved to Colombia or Peru somewhere. Anyway, we never had enough evidence on her to put her away."

Agent Davis sat back down in his chair, intrigued by everything he didn't know about the Milano family. Davis had come to this division of the FBI shortly after the Milano era so he really didn't know much about them. Flint sat there and gave him the complete run down bringing him on board with everything he knew.

When Flint was asked about Sosa, he didn't have the slightest idea who that was. He only knew a couple of names, mainly those of importance like Gio, Semaj, Bonjo, and Ortiz. He really didn't know Sosa, LuLu, Jah Jah, and Marcela that well, but he heard about the work they put in for the family.

"Semaj Richardson," Davis mumbled to himself after Agent Flint walked off. "I think this might be Sosa," he told Agent Mason.

"How can we be sure?" Mason asked, reaching over and grabbing her picture off the screen.

"Well, I think that at this point we have to find her and watch her every move. When she slips up, we'll be right there," Davis answered, once again getting up from his chair and heading out of the office.

"Make sure you take care of my cousin," Semaj said, carrying Nyala into Santos's house.

There really wasn't any need to tell him that because Semaj had several of her men watching his house around the clock. She made it so that they were unnoticed in order to give Sosa and Santos some space, but there was no way in hell Semaj was going to leave her vulnerable. Sosa was way too important to be left alone.

"You don't have to worry about it. I'ma keep her safe," Santos promised, walking up behind Semaj as she was tucking Nyala in her bed.

Sosa walked into the room at the tail end of what Santos had said. "Keep who safe?" Sosa questioned, walking up and putting her arms around him.

"You and Nyala," he answered, kissing her on the forehead. "I swear on my life," he assured.

Semaj smiled, shaking her head. This was the first time she saw Sosa being this close with a man. She and Semaj could tell by the look in Santos's eyes that he meant every word he said. He kind of reminded her of someone whom she knew loved her in the same manner. For a minute, she got carried away in her own thoughts thinking about Qua.

"Who you thinking about?" Sosa asked,

tapping Semaj on her arm, snapping her out of her trance.

Semaj was zoned out so much she didn't even notice Santos leaving the room. "Shit girl, you don't even have to tell me. I know that look from anywhere," Sosa smiled.

"I'm so confused right now, Sosa. Every time I get around him that boy do something to me. I keep tryin' to tell myself that I'm getting married, but nothing seems to work. He breaks down every barrier, every guard, and every wall I try to put up," Semaj confided.

"Well, did you try to tell him how you feel?"

"I was going to, but he's mad as hell at me right now. I asked him was he working with the police," Semaj told her.

Sosa's jaw dropped. Even she wouldn't believe Qua would work for the police. He was the type of nigga that had pride and stood by the street code to the letter.

"So what are you gonna do?"

Semaj smiled then threw her arm around Sosa, leading her out of the room. "I'ma take my confused ass back to my dad's house and get some sleep." She laughed, heading down the steps.

Tomorrow was gonna be a long day for the members of the 16 Tent. A lot of issues needed to be discussed, and Sosa's return was highly anticipated. There was going to be a lot of questions that needed to be answered concerning her abduction in the jungle. When something like this happened to one of the members, everybody wanted to know what they could do to help bring some type of retribution to the individuals responsible.

Qua had driven around all night looking for Ron. He had been missing in action after the failed exchange with Semaj the other day. Ron wasn't answering his phone nor was he at any of the spots he frequented in the hood. Qua went to the only place he hadn't which was Ron's mom's house. She lived in the cut, out in Albany, New York, in the suburbs. It was about an hour drive from the city, but Qua didn't mind. It didn't even seem like an hour to Qua because the whole way there, he was processing all the events that took place over the past few weeks. He more so focused on Ron's behavior and how nervous and suspicious he'd looked at times. Some of the things he did were equivalent to that of an informant, and the one thing that stuck out the most was how constantly he asked about Sosa. Her name came out of his mouth a little too much.

When Qua drove down Cedar Brook Road, he looked at the many cars parked in their respected driveways and others that were parked on the street. None of the cars resembled anything that

Ron drove and when Qua pulled into Ms. Wahida's empty driveway he knew for sure that Ron wasn't there.

"Damn nigga, where da hell are you?" Qua mumbled to himself, reaching over and grabbing his phone from the passenger seat.

He went through his contact list and tried to call Ron again. He got the same results: Ron's phone went straight to voicemail. Irritation turned into frustration quick. He looked around before getting out of his car and walking up to Ms. Wahida's door. Qua wanted to be sure Ron wasn't hiding out inside.

Ms. Wahida came to the door three seconds after Qua rang the doorbell. She had a good amount of energy from the moment she greeted him.

"Yo' punk ass ain't been up here in months," Ms. Wahida joked, stepping to the side so Qua could enter. "If you lookin' for that irresponsible son of mine, you might wanna wait in line. His ass was suppose to bring me some money for my bills," she complained.

Qua couldn't do nothing, but laugh at her. Ms. Wahida was hood for real and she wasn't ashamed of it, even when Ron moved her to an upscale community. She just brought her hood life with her.

"I been lookin' all over for dis nigga, Ms. Wahida. The last time I talked to him we was tryin' to figure out a way to get you to take chemo," Qua said, walking over to the mantel and picking up a picture of Ron when he was a baby.

"Chemo? What in the hell I need with chemo?" Ms. Wahida shot back with her hands on her hips. "I know you ain't let that boy run that cancer trick on you." She laughed. "I haven't heard that one since he was in high school and security caught him getting high in the bathroom. He told them that I had cancer so they wouldn't bother me with suspending him," Ms. Wahida said.

Qua put his head down and shook it, remembering that day clearly. He couldn't believe he let Ron get that one off on him. Now things were becoming clearer and the possibility of Ron being an informant seemed evident. But the love Qua had for his friend didn't allow him to believe it.

"Ms. Wahida, if Ron come out here, please tell him to call me," Qua said, digging in his pocket and pulling out a wad of money.

He gave her about eleven hundred dollars, then left. He couldn't stand to be around Ms. Wahida with how mad he was at Ron, and the one thing he would always have for Ms. Wahida no matter what, is respect.

"Is that his Range Rover right there?" Agent Mason

asked, pointing across the street.

Davis looked down at the GPS tracker then back up at the Range Rover. The device was telling him that the GPS was right there in the vicinity.

"Yeah, that's his," Davis said, pulling over and parking at the top of the block.

Davis and Mason both got out of the Crown Victoria and looked around. The street was pretty much empty, only having about six houses on the block. Everything else was vacant lots and a couple abandoned houses.

"What house do you think he's in?"

"I don't know, but we're gonna find out," Davis said, walking over and picking up a piece of rock from the sidewalk. "Check it out," he said, throwing the rock at the back window.

When the glass shattered, it caused the alarm to go off. It blared loudly in the night, echoing up and down the street. Davis and Mason both backed up into one of the vacant lots and waited. It didn't take long for Ron to come running out of one of the houses with his jeans halfway pulled up, no t-shirt on, and with a gun in his hand. Now Davis and Mason had to take a more stern approach.

"FBI! FBI! Put the gun down," Davis yelled as he and Mason came out of the lot with their weapons drawn.

Ron spun around and was about to raise his gun, but Davis yelled out again. "Put the gun down,

Ron," he shouted as he crossed the street.

It's one thing to feel like you bold enough to have a shootout with the police but it's a totally different story when you're smack dab in the middle of the situation and it's actually about to go down. The last thing a nigga wanna do is get aired out by the police. Ron wasn't built for that, not now and not ever. He dropped his gun and put his hands on top of his head.

"Y'all didn't have to fuck my Range up," Ron said, while being patted down by Mason.

"Yeah well, next time you might wanna think about that when you decide to disappear."

Davis picked up the Glock .40 Ron had thrown down, lifting it in the air by the butt. "You love pissing me off don't you," Davis said, passing the gun to Mason who had pulled a handkerchief out of his pocket.

It wasn't any secret to where the gun was going, right in the back seat of the Crown Victoria with the rest of the evidence that was confiscated from Ron. Davis just piled it on and the only way that it was going to disappear was if Ron continued to play ball with them.

"Take a ride with us, Ron," Davis said, pushing his back into the direction of the car.

Semaj was riding alone in her Aston Vanquish

looking in the rearview mirror to see if her guards were still following close behind. It was 12:30 at night and the only person she could think about was Qua. She didn't mean to disrespect him the way that she did and felt as though it needed to be fixed. The only problem was, he wasn't answering her phone calls so that she could apologize.

"Fuck it, I know where you at," Semaj said aloud, taking the top half of her seat belt and putting it behind her back.

Semaj looked in the rearview again, but his time, she opened up the V-12 engine like she was a racecar driver. The highway was empty except for a few cars that were out, making it easy for Semaj to punch it to 120 mph in seconds. The two Tahoe trucks her men were in didn't stand a chance in keeping up with her and didn't even attempt to once they saw her car getting smaller and smaller. Within two minutes, she had disappeared into the night.

It took Semaj every bit of 25 minutes to get to Qua's condo in downtown Manhattan. When she got into the building's garage, she pulled out her phone and tried to call him. The phone just rang until it went to voicemail. She knew he had to be there because both his Benz and his BMW were in the garage.

Semaj was determined to clean up the mess she made in hopes that she could save their friendship at the very least. That's one thing she didn't want to lose and would do just about anything to assure that it stayed intact.

It wasn't hard for Semaj to get past security in the lobby. A cute face and a nice body could still get you a pass once in awhile.

Knock! Knock! Knock! Semaj stood back and waited for Qua to come to the door. The whole way up on the elevator she prayed that he didn't have one of his hoochies with him. It would have been an awkward moment for her.

After seeing that he wasn't answering, Semaj turned on her heels and was about to leave. Then she heard the locks on the door clicking. She stopped and turned back around. Qua opened the door with a half-sleepy look in his face and a black Desert Eagle in his hand. He only had on a pair of sweat pants, showing off his chiseled stomach and muscular chest. Even his feet were properly manicured. Nobody could deny that Qua kept his shit on point.

"Its 1:20 in the mornin', Maj. You either here to kill me or get fucked," Qua said, grabbing a handful of his dick through his sweats.

Semaj blushed. She hadn't been talked to like that in a long time, especially by Qua. She been gone so long she forgot how sexy a hood nigga sounded talking dirty.

"Can we talk?" she asked, leaning against the

wall.

"Yeah, in the mornin'," Qua said, stepping to the side, eyeing her.

She put her head down, smiling. Semaj wasn't fooling anybody though. From the moment Qua opened his door she had thoughts of giving him some pussy. She couldn't even get her words together standing there in front of him, and for what it was worth, she didn't have to because Qua was at the end of his rope.

He reached out and grabbed the bottom of Semaj's jacket, pulling her through the door. She didn't put up a fight either. It was as if she had no control over what her body was doing. She walked up to Qua with her head down, submissive and humble, the way he always made her feel.

Qua lifted her chin up and looked her in the eyes. He didn't have to say a word, and he didn't. He leaned in and pressed his lips against hers, pulling her body closer to his. Semaj just let herself go, returning his kisses as she reached up and placed her hand on the side of his face.

Qua finally came up for air to close the front door. He grabbed Semaj's hand and led her to his bedroom. Semaj thought that she would be scared or nervous, but she wasn't. Piece by piece, Qua released Semaj's clothes until she stood before him with only her lace bra and panties on. He grabbed her by the waist and lifted her up to place her on his bed. She crawled backwards on her elbows until she reached the center of the bed. Qua climbed on top of her, lifting her legs up to strip her of the blue satin panties she had on. He kissed her softly from her calf, down to the back of her thigh until he reached her wet insides. He ate Semaj's pussy until her body couldn't take it anymore. Within seconds, he made her cum. He sucked, licked, and swallowed every morsel of her fluids, leaving her body shaking.

Qua grabbed her thighs and pulled her body down to him. She didn't even notice that his sweatpants were off; and before she could ask him to use a condom, Qua slid his rock-hard dick inside of her.

"Hmmmmm," Semaj moaned, taking him inside of her.

It was no offense to Vikingo's dick, but Qua was hung well, and he knew how to work it. The way he slowly slid in and out of her made Semaj remember everything. She remembered how gentle Qua used to be with her body, and how much attention he paid to what pleased her. She remembered how he used to fuck her like a porn star then turn around and make love to her like a gentlemen.

"I love you, Maj," Qua told her, looking her in the eyes.

Semaj said what only came natural to her when she was caught up in Qua's web. "I love you, too," she whispered right before grabbing the back of his head and shoving her tongue into his mouth.

Tonight, Qua wasn't fucking at all. He missed Semaj so much and couldn't wait for the opportunity to be back inside of her. Qua was going to take his time and get reacquainted with the only woman he'd ever loved. He planned to make love to Semaj all night, something both he and she needed.

Visions of Semaj walking down the aisle in a beautiful white gown flashed through Vikingo's mind as he slept. In his dream, he stood at the altar watching as she made her way to him. The dream was so real Vikingo managed to grin in his sleep.

Like most dreams do, Vikingo's switched up without his permission, taking him straight to his honeymoon. Semaj was under the covers giggling as Vikingo came out of the bathroom. He slowly made his way over to the bed to consummate his marriage and when he pulled back the covers, Semaj had her legs spread apart, Qua was on top of her, and he was pounding away. Semaj looked up at Vikingo and said, "It's his pussy."

Vikingo's heart monitor went erratic; his breathing became heavy, and his head shifted from side to side. The dream hurt so bad it woke him up and it was at that point Vikingo knew that something was wrong.

Chapter 5

Two heavily armed men opened the 15-foot double doors to the Old Steel warehouse and stepped to the side so that two black Lincoln Town Cars could enter. The 16 Tent meeting was taking place here and the security was tighter than it's ever been. Considering what happened at the Four Seasons hotel, everybody was a little on edge.

Wong Won was already in the building, dressed in an all white Armani suit and a pair of brown Tom Ford shoes. He sat at the long wooden table with three of his men standing behind him, two more by the door, and another three standing outside by the cars. All of his men were armed with submachine guns and 50 round clips.

"I hope this will be fast, I want to go home," Marco said, walking over to the table from the Lincoln Town Car he just arrived in.

His men had guns in their hands nobody in the room would be able to identify. They looked futuristic. The only thing that was important to Marco was that had a shootout occurred, his men would be in a better position than everybody else. The small machine guns didn't even look like they carried 100 shot rounds, but they did, and strapped to each and every one of their vests were two extra clips. They had more than enough bullets to slaughter a small country.

Semaj stood on a platform that wrapped around the entire warehouse some 25 feet above ground level, looking down on everyone sitting at the table. Nobody even noticed her until she began to speak.

"The 16 Tent was built on many things, but there were several key pillars that solidified the foundation," Semaj yelled out from above.

Everyone stopped what he or she was doing and looked up. Semaj leaned off of the rail and began walking the short distance down towards the steps.

"Honor! Respect! Loyalty!" she continued, as she came towards them. "For anyone who violates these pillars, the punishment of death is prescribed, in accordance to the agreement of each family who gave their blood oath to the Tent," she said.

It wasn't until she got to the bottom of the steps that everyone noticed she had a gun in her hand; a 17 Glock 9mm to be exact. She stood at the head of the table, leaning over it with the gun in her hand rested vertically on top. She stared at Wong, Ezra, and Marco sitting there staring back at her.

"We have a traitor in the Tent. One who tried to kill me on several different occasions, but failed. This person conspired with another Tent member to assassinate me and take over my land in Colombia," Semaj stated.

"Don't you think we need to wait for the rest of the members to get here before we discuss this any further?" Marco asked, pulling out a cigar from his inside blazer pocket.

On cue, four hard bangs on the large double doors got everybody's attention. Semaj's two men walked over and swung the doors open. Two black Tahoes pulled into the warehouse, parking right next to Marco's car. Sosa, Mitch, Qua, and Penny hopped out of the first Tahoe, but only Mitch and Sosa joined the other members at the table.

"Good to see you, Sosa," Ezra said, nodding his head at her.

"You're one tough cookie," Wong Won pointed, giving Sosa a wink of the eye.

Marco didn't say a word. He just smiled and lit his cigar, blowing the heavy smoke in the air. Where he was from, women went through a lot worse than what Sosa experienced on a daily basis, so he wasn't impressed.

"Where's Nikolai?" Marco wanted to know,

taking another tote of his cigar.

Semaj left from the table and walked over to the second Tahoe. With her gun still in hand, she opened the back door and motioned for Nikolai to get out of the truck. She did, climbing out and adjusting her clothes before walking over to the table. Semaj walked behind her. Ezra and Wong had a confused look on their faces, wondering what was going on.

"For the record, this bitch is holding me here against my will," Nikolai said, taking a seat at the table.

Ezra, Marco, and Wong looked from Nikolai to Semaj. "Is this true?" Wong Won asked.

"Yes, it's true," Semaj answered. "I caught Nikolai—"

"You didn't catch me doing anything," Nikolai snapped, cutting Semaj off.

"I have proof you was trying to kill me," Semaj retorted. "You turned around and killed Raul because you knew that he had told me, and now you wanna hop on Marco's jet and go back to Russia. I don't think so. You're not going anywhere and as soon as I present my proof to the rest of the family, I'm gonna take pleasure in putting a bullet in yo' head," Semaj made clear.

Everybody at the table sat in silence for a moment. Ezra and Wong needed to process everything that Semaj was claiming. It was a very serious violation to kill another Tent member, but it was just as bad to make false accusations on another member that could possibly have them removed or even killed.

"These are serious charges, Semaj. What kind of proof will you be presenting?" Wong questioned.

Semaj kept her eyes on Nikolai the whole time before answering. "I'm working on something. But I'll have the proof I need very soon."

Semaj thought back to Raul revealing to her the conversation he had recorded between him and Nikolai plotting to kill her. She had been trying to crack his four-digit password in order to gain access to the phone's voicemail, where the conversation was stored. She was convinced that she was very close to getting the password.

"I think that a suitable time frame should be in order for Semaj to present her proof," Marco suggested.

"Yes, I agree. Nikolai can't continue to be held against her will," Wong Won added.

"I think 48 hours is more than enough time. I'll see to it that Nikolai won't leave New York," Marco said, putting his cigar out on the table.

"Wait, wait. Is that gonna be enough time?" Sosa asked Semaj.

Semaj thought about Raul's cell phone that she was keeping very close to her and then looked at the members of the Tent. She really believed that in 48 hours, she could figure out the four-digit code to Raul's phone. She nodded her head at Sosa to confirm the time allotted.

"Alright, so it's agreed upon. Semaj has 48 hours to present her proof to the Tent. If not, then Nikolai is free to go," Wong Won announced.

He looked around the room for the final confirmation. Marco nodded, Sosa nodded, Mitch nodded, and Ezra nodded making it official, but not complete.

"Semaj, you are aware of the consequences if you cannot produce this proof?" Ezra asked, wanting to make sure Semaj fully understood the position she had put herself in.

Ezra didn't even have to go there. Semaj was well aware that if she could not prove what she accused Nikolai of, she could be removed from the 16 Tent; and 9 times out of 10, that's what would happen. It was a risk Semaj was willing to take in order to assure her safety, and even if she didn't get the code she had made up her mind Nikolai wasn't going to leave New York alive.

Chapter 6

"Alright, Nyala, it's time for bed," Santos announced coming into her room.

It was a huge step for Sosa to entrust Santos with watching over Nyala while she helped Semaj out with her situation. A lot was taken into consideration, but the most important factor was that Sosa had fallen in love with Santos and trusted him with her own life. The second reason was just as important and that was the fact that Nyala actually liked Santos. Sosa never saw her gravitate to any man, not even Ox, her biological father.

"I have to go to the bathroom first," Nyala happily told Santos as she jumped from the bed and into his arms.

"A'ight, a'ight, but make it quick. Mommy will kill both of us if she come home and see you still awake this late on a school night," Santos said, putting Nyala down so she could run to the bathroom.

While he still had a little bit of time Santos shot downstairs to grab the rest of the clean clothes he folded up after they came out of the dryer. Over the past few days Sosa turned him into a househusband. Most of the chores he did voluntarily, mainly because he enjoyed the family atmosphere, something he didn't have growing up.

"Nyala! I'll be up there in two minutes," he shouted, walking into the dining room where the pile of clothes was.

Santos was unaware that somebody other than him and Nyala was in the house. The screen door in the kitchen was cracked open, but since he didn't walk into the kitchen when he came downstairs, Santos was unaware of it.

When Santos left the dining room and walked into the living room, he was startled by Patrick who came out of nowhere. He was standing at the bottom of the steps with his hand rested on the butt of his gun tucked in his waist.

"Is Sosa here?" Patrick asked in a low voice, cutting his eyes up the steps.

"Who da fuck is you?" Santos snapped back, putting the clothes he had in his hand, onto the couch.

Santos stepped a little closer, prompting Patrick to pull his weapon out and point it at him. Santos was a little too far back to try and wrestle the gun away from him so all he could do was stand there.

"I'm not gonna ask you again," Patrick spoke.

"Nah, she left, and I don't know when she's coming back," Santos answered.

That's all Patrick needed to hear. If Sosa was somewhere in the house she wasn't gonna just let Patrick walk out of there with Nyala. Seeing as she wasn't home it made his job easier. It wasn't even necessary for Santos to be standing around any longer and Patrick definitely wasn't going to give him a chance to play hero.

Patrick pulled the trigger without a second thought, sending a hot led ball right at Santos's chest. The bullet hit him right over his right nipple, dropping him to the ground. Nyala heard the shot and froze at the bathroom door. She was afraid to move thinking back to the time when she was caught in the middle of a shootout between Sosa and Paris at Ox's house in Jamaica.

Nyala quietly closed the bathroom door and hid in the cabinets under the sink. She could hear footsteps coming up the stairs and from how heavy they sounded; she knew that it wasn't Santos. Patrick walked up and down the hallway, checking each and every room. Nobody was in them and if it wasn't for Santos calling Nyala's name out, he might have thought that Nyala wasn't there. But Patrick knew she was there and the only place he didn't check was the bathroom, and as he walked up to the door and saw that it was locked, he was more than sure that Nyala was in there.

"Maj, we got less than 40 hours and you still playin' with that phone. Why don't we just kill da bitch and be done with it," Qua said, walking over and taking a seat next to her on the couch.

Back in the day Semaj was like a phone hacker. Every boyfriend she had, she managed to gain access to his voicemail account. If she sat there long enough, she would eventually punch in the right password. The only difference about Raul's phone was that she didn't know anything about him pertaining to numbers. She didn't know his birthday, social security number, driver's license number, license plate number, or anything of the sort. Even still, Semaj sat there and continued punching in numbers randomly.

"If killing her was that easy I would have done that. We have to try and do it the right way," Semaj said, looking into Raul's phone screen.

"Semaj, look at me," Qua said, putting his hand over the phone. "We need to find another way," he told Semaj, getting her to look at him. "If need be, I'll take full responsibility for killing her so that they won't kick you out of the Tent."

Semaj looked over at Qua and smiled. She

could never get enough of seeing how far he would go for her. That's one thing she loved about Qua. He never had a problem showing his love and if it ever came down to it, he would sacrifice his life for her without a second thought.

"Damn, boy you know I lo...."

Semaj stopped mid-sentence as an idea hit her like a Mack truck. "Hold on for one second," she said, looking back into Raul's phone.

The first Tent meeting Raul came to, he brought his sister with him to represent Cuba. Semaj couldn't remember the woman's name, but it was on the tip of her tongue. She had only come to one meeting, then Raul convinced her that she didn't need to come to the meetings anymore, so she stopped coming.

"What are you doing?"

"Shhhhhh," she motioned, going through Raul's phone book. "Selina?" she questioned herself, not really sure if that was Raul's sister's name on the screen.

There was only one way to find out and that was by calling the number, which Semaj did. The phone rang several times before a female answered it.

"¿Porque no me as llamado?" Selina asked, wondering why Raul hadn't called her in a few days.

She didn't even know that he was dead yet. After he sent her back to Cuba, Raul had her taking care of business at home and taking her focus off what was going on in the States.

"*No hablo ingles,*" Semaj told her, not really being in the mood to speak in Spanish right now.

"Who is this, and why are you calling me from my brother's phone?" Selina questioned, walking out on her balcony.

"Your brother is dead," Semaj told her flat out. "You may or may not remember me from the 16 Tent meeting we had in Australia."

Selina sat there stunned by what Semaj just told her about her brother. She took the phone away from her ear and looked into the night sky. Raul wasn't just her brother, he was her best friend, and probably the reason why she was the person she was today.

"Are you still there?" Semaj asked, hearing the silence on the other end of the phone. "My name is—"

"Yeah, I know who you are," Selina said, cutting her off. "So I guess you're calling to tell me that you was the one who killed Raul."

All Selina could think about was the day Raul told her that they were going to kill Semaj. She tried to stop him, but it was too late and this was the consequence to his actions.

"I didn't kill your brother, Selina, but I know who did, and I need you to help me prove it," Semaj said in a calm voice.

"What are you talking about?" Selina asked, looking back into the house where her mother was watching TV in her chair.

Semaj had to minimize what she could say over the phone, having said enough as it was, but she did explain briefly about her need to gain access to Raul's voicemail. When she asked Selina if she knew the four-digit code, Selina hung up on her.

"Hello! Hello!" Semaj yelled into the phone. "She hung up on me," Semaj told Qua, who was sitting there staring at her.

"She didn't give you the code?" Qua asked.

"No, but I got a feeling that she knows it," Semaj said, grabbing her phone off the table in front of the couch.

She scrolled through her phone until she came across Gonzalez's number. He was always on call and on point when Semaj needed him. He answered the phone on the second ring.

"*Oye Señorita,*" Gonzalez answered. "What can I do for you?"

"I need you to get a crew together. We're going to Cuba. I should be arriving in about three hours," Semaj said, looking at her watch.

"*Si, Señorita,*" was all Gonzalez said before Semaj ended the call.

Semaj jumped up from the couch and headed to her room. Qua was on her heels. "I'm coming with you," he said, watching as Semaj packed a few things.

She stopped doing what she was doing when she heard him say that. She walked over and stood in front of him. As bad as she would have liked for him to come with her, she couldn't let him. She did have that much respect for Vikingo not to bring the man whom she had an affair with to their home and around his people.

There were still things Semaj had to talk to Qua about concerning her infidelities and how wrong it was for her to have slept with him while she was engaged to Vikingo. It was something that bothered her from the time she woke up that morning. Because of the current situation with the Tent, she was unable to get around to discussing it with him. For now, Semaj had to go take care of her business and there was no way in hell Qua was going to be able to come. It simply wouldn't be right.

Murda Mitch turned onto a street that was full of cops as he was driving Sosa home. Sosa leaned up in her seat trying to figure out whose house they were at. "What da hell," Sosa said, seeing that they were at Santos's house.

"Pull over! Pull over!" she shouted at Mitch,

opening the passenger side door before the car even came to a complete stop.

Mitch jumped out of the car and they both darted down the street towards Santos's house. The cops stopped both of them before they could get across the lawn. At the same time, Santos was being taken out of the house in a gurney.

"My daughter is in there!" Sosa yelled at the cops. "My daughter!"

"There's nobody else in the house, ma'am. A detective will be over here shortly to speak to you," the one cop told her.

She broke away from him and ran over to the EMTs who were rolling Santos over to the ambulance. They were still working on him; giving him CPR, applying pressure to the wound and pushing fluids through the I.V. into his body. Sosa broke down at the sight of it. Mitch was there to grab her before she dropped to the ground.

"Nyala!" she yelled, breaking away from Mitch and running towards the house.

She ran right into the arms of the detective who was coming out of the house. "Get off me. My daughter is in there!" she cried out.

"There's nobody else in the house. What is your daughter's name?" the detective asked.

"Her name is Nyala," Sosa cried out.

She was tired and weak at this point and was at the brink of an anxiety attack. The more she thought about it, the more she knew who was behind it. She couldn't believe she had forgotten about Ox's people trying to take Nyala away from her. She was sick and the more she thought about it, the lighter her head got. Right in the mist of her trying to give her name to the detective, she passed out right into Mitch's arms.

Semaj convinced Qua to stay back and keep an eye on Nikolai and the rest of the Tent members until she got back. He was also given access to all of the men Semaj had in the city. With her guards and Qua's own crew of young gunners, he had more than enough manpower to hold every member of the Tent at bay.

Qua looked down at the key Semaj gave him before she left the condo to fly back to Cuba. The key was to a storage unit in the Bronx that had his original shipment of 500 kilos in it. She convinced him to take it because she wasn't going to be able to distribute any more coke to the East Coast until this situation was taken care of. That meant Qua was going to make a killing in the city for a minute.

As Qua sat in his car, looking out into the night, his cell phone almost vibrated off the dashboard. He reached up and grabbed it in the nick of time. He looked at the screen and saw that it was Ron.

"Damn my nigga, where da fuck you been at?"

"I been chillin', gettin' my situation together, my dude. I need to holla at you, too," Ron said. "The streets need us right now," he spoke.

"Yeah, I know. I'm on right now, too. That's why I been tryin' to catch up wit you," Qua said, trying to play it off like he wasn't mad at him right now. "I'm on my way to you right now. Where you at son?" Qua asked, reaching under his seat and pulling out a chrome .45 automatic.

Ron gave him his location, which was somewhere in Brooklyn. It didn't matter where he was, Qua was on his way there. A lot of questions needed to be answered and if Ron couldn't give the right response Qua wasn't going to have a problem leaving Ron where he stood.

They were like family, but once you cross the lines, Qua didn't see the love anymore. The same way he would deal with an average nigga on the streets, Qua would deal with Ron.

Chapter 7

Instead of a second ambulance being called to take Sosa to the hospital, the detective that was on the scene took her himself. Mitch followed behind them the whole way there. Sosa wasn't admitted, but given medicine for her anxiety attack. She was back up and walking around in a short period of time.

"We gon' find her, I promise you," Mitch told Sosa as she walked up to him standing outside of the operating room where Santos was.

Santos's condition was critical, but stable. The bullet tore through his chest and was lodged right above his lung. Surgery to remove the bullet was underway and doctors were hopeful that no further damage would occur during the surgery. All Sosa could do was wait until Santos woke up, so that he could let her know what had happened or possibly where they took Nyala.

"Semaj ain't answering her phone," Sosa said,

looking down at her iPhone.

"She still might be in the air right now. Give me a few minutes and I'll give her cousin down there a call and tell her to tell Semaj to call me as soon as she lands," Mitch told Sosa.

Sosa was stressed out. All she wanted was Nyala back and the people responsible for her abduction to die. Ox's family had finally got Sosa to her breaking point, so much so that as of right now she was considering going to Jamaica and killing everybody left in the bloodline. She felt like that was the only way they would stop coming for her daughter. First and foremost, before anything could happen, Sosa had to find Nyala and the only person that was capable of doing that was getting a bullet taken out of his chest. Again, all she could do was to wait.

"Is this room secure?" Nikolai asked Marco, as she entered his hotel room.

Since Marco volunteered to make sure Nikolai stayed in New York, it was only befitting that she stayed in the same hotel with him, of course in different rooms.

"Yes, talk freely. I had the room swept for bugs five times," Marco answered, walking over to the mini bar. "Do you have any idea how she plans to prove that you was trying to kill her?"

"We! How she plans on proving that *we*, tried to have her killed," Nikolai replied, quickly trying to remind Marco that he had a hand in the assassination attempt as well.

Marco threw back a shot of scotch, then cut his eyes over at Nikolai who took a seat on his couch. He had a feeling she was gonna try and pull him back into it once it got ugly. He wasn't too worried about it because he had backed out early on, so his verbal and physical actions were limited to the point where he could deny anything and everything, if Nikolai did try and play that card. He wasn't even gonna entertain her last comment.

"So, I hope you have a plan B instead of just sitting here," Marco inquired. "You know that if she does come back with some type of proof, they are going to kill you," he said.

"Nobody's gonna kill me," Nikolai snapped back. "If I die, everybody dies," she said, with a serious look on her face.

She wasn't too happy about the threat of death, but it was true and she knew it. If she were in Russia, she'd be able to avoid it by going on the run. But she was in New York City and had all eyes on her, and not just Marco's.

Ezra had his men watching her every move. Wong Won had some of his men watching her, and Semaj had Qua and her people watching her. For the next 35 hours, Nikolai couldn't take a shit without everybody knowing what she ate for dinner. The crazy thing was, while everybody was watching her, she had people watching Semaj. She was a couple steps ahead of her, knowing what move Semaj was gonna make next.

"I need one thing from you and then you can be done with me," Nikolai said, getting up from the couch.

"Yeah, and what's that?"

"I think you know what I need," she said, giving him a devious look.

Marco could see the devil in her eyes. He knew that she was up to something and he knew exactly what she wanted from him. Nikolai's back was up against the wall right now, and her only way out was doing what she did best.

Qua pulled up to the Redtop storage facility and parked. He waited for a few minutes until Ron's Range Rover pulled up and parked right behind Qua's— he looked around for anything suspicious. Ron got out looking around in the same manner.

"What up, son," Ron greeted, walking up to Qua, sticking his hand out for a dap.

He got within five feet of Qua and then the unexpected happened. At first Qua thought that his cell phone was going off the way it vibrated in his jacket pocket, but when he pulled the little black pager out, he threw his head back in frustration.

"Damn my nigga, you got a beeper," Ron joked, looking down at it.

Qua had to go along with it. He couldn't tell Ron that what he had in his hand was a device that goes off when someone with a wire on them gets within five feet of it. Now he knew that Ron was wearing a wire and he had to be careful what he said and did, knowing that the police on the other side of that wire were somewhere in the vicinity.

"So wassup? Did you score from ol' girl?" Ron asked, leaning up against Qua's car next to him.

"Nah, brah. I didn't do nothing wit' homegirl. I'm chillin' out right now," Qua told him, tucking the vibrating pager back into his jacket pocket.

"Damn, my dude. She suppose to have them 500 kilos on deck. Why did she roll out yesterday?" Ron asked, trying to get Qua to talk.

Qua didn't have much rap for Ron. In fact, he felt like blowin' Ron's head clean off his shoulders. Qua hated rats in every sense of the word. He despised them and thought that they all should die.

"You know what son, I love you my nigga," Qua said, resting his right hand on the butt of his gun.

Ron didn't even notice it since he was on Qua's left side. The longer Ron sat there talking crazy, the more upset Qua became. He took the safety off his gun and continued to look around, contemplating whether or not he could shoot Ron in his head and get away before the cops on the other side of that wire could get to him.

Ron just kept talking and talking about the shipment and the new connect, along with the aspects of their business. At this point, Qua was pretty much beyond disgusted by his actions. He pulled the black .45 automatic from his waist and held it down by his thigh. He scanned the area one last time to see if he could see anything. Ron was talking so much, he didn't even notice Qua had drawn his weapon. It wasn't until Qua turned around to face him, that Ron saw the gun.

"Yo son, what's the gun for?" Ron asked with his face twisted up like he was mad.

"Nigga, you a rat?" Qua asked, gripping the gun tighter. "Where it at?" he said, reaching out and patting Ron's chest.

Ron leaned against the car and put his hands in the air as though he was consenting to the weak pat down. Ron was still shocked to see the gun was out, and he was even more shocked when Qua pointed it at his chest.

"We gotta get him out of there," Agent Mason said, leaning in to start the car.

Agent Davis reached out and stopped him before he could turn the key in the ignition.

They had been sitting there listening to the whole conversation, but Davis was a little more experienced in this field to know not to jump the gun so fast.

"Relax, partner. He's not gonna shoot him," Davis said, taking the headphones off of his head.

"You sure? 'Cause it damn sure sounded like it to me," Mason replied in a concerned manner.

"Listen, if Qua was gonna shoot him, he would have already done it. These two guys have been best friends since they were toddlers. No way he's gonna be able to pull the trigger and I know that slick talkin' muthafucka is gonna find a way out of this," Davis said, putting his headset back on his ears.

"I don't think you wanna do dat, homie," Ron said, shaking his head. "The feds gon' bury you under the ground if you pull dat trigger," he continued, lowering his hands with the assurance that Qua wasn't going to shoot him. "Look homie, dis shit ain't about you. They just want Sosa," he tried to explain.

Qua wasn't trying to hear anything coming out of his mouth. Not only was he a rat, he just sat there and admitted to it like it wasn't nothing. Qua hated that the most and it hurt more because it was coming from Ron.

"You dead to me, nigga. If you even come back around me again, I swear on my motha I'ma blow ya fuckin' head off. I don't give a fuck if the feds is listening or not," Qua threatened, pressing the gun against his solar plexus.

He still thought about shooting Ron, but ultimately decided not to. There were more important and pressing issues Qua had to deal with, sitting in jail wasn't going to benefit Semaj at all. For those reasons alone Qua lowered his gun, pushed Ron to the side, then got into his car and pulled off.

"Hi, are you here for Mr. Torres?" the doctor came out and asked Sosa and Mitch, who were sitting in the waiting room.

"Yes, is he okay?" Sosa asked, rising to her feet.

"Ma'am, Mr. Torres is a survivor. The bullet was successfully removed and he is in stable condition. Miraculously, he's awake. He's groggy from the pain medication, but he's awake. The nurses are about to transport him over to the recovery unit, so you should be able to talk to him shortly" the doctor explained before walking away.

Sosa was glad that he was all right. Even though he was unable to stop the abduction, Sosa was grateful that he took a bullet trying to protect her little girl. For him to come away with his life was a big deal in itself, considering Sosa knew the kind of people who were behind it. Normally, Ox's people wouldn't leave a living witness around to tell any story. When they shoot, they shoot to kill and most of the time it is headshots only.

"So, we're just gonna let him go?" Agent Mason asked Davis. "If Qua does know who Sosa is, he's gonna tip her or him off. At this point, we think Sosa might be a woman, but we don't know for sure yet."

"I'm banking on that. Start the car," Davis said, putting his headset back on. "Stay a nice distance behind him, but don't lose him."

Davis and Mason's cover was blown, but Davis knew how to make good out of a bad situation. Had he locked Qua up right then and there, they wouldn't have enough evidence to charge him with anything, so he would have been right back out on the streets. Carrying a firearm without a license alone was a state beef and not federal. Qua would have bailed out on those charges within an hour of being in the precinct.

The thing Davis was banking on was for Qua to either call Sosa or lead him straight to him or her. If he called, Davis would know because Qua's phone was tapped and every number that he dialed was recorded, along with the conversation he was having. It would have been even better if

Qua would lead Davis to Sosa. Not only would he be able to see what Sosa looked like, Davis would also be able to link Qua to Sosa for indictment purposes.

In the end, all wasn't lost. The only thing that changed was the fact that Davis and Mason were on Qua's heels now instead of Ron's. Of course they could continue to track Ron, but it probably would serve no purpose, considering that after tonight his name wouldn't be any good in the city of New York.

Chapter 8

Time was of the essence and Semaj couldn't afford to waste a second of it. She flew straight to Cuba on a private jet, which only took a few hours. When she landed in Havana's airport, security was tight. She knew that it was going to be like that anyway, so she took the liberty of not bringing any weapons, just Gonzalez and a few of his men.

"It's going to be about a 45-minute drive from here, *Señorita*," Gonzalez informed Semaj, as he placed a couple of duffle bags he brought along, into the trunk of the rental car.

Gonzalez had family in Cuba so it wasn't that hard for him to call in a favor and get a crew together for the day; knowing that they were going to be compensated heavily by Semaj for their services also made it worth their while. The men selected for the job weren't as tactical as the man Gonzalez had back in Colombia, but they were sufficient enough to get the job done.

"Now, I've never been to this town, *Señorita,* but my nephew said that it's run by the Ordoñez family. They control a nice fraction of the drug-trading business in Cuba and they are feared by most cartels in the country," Gonzalez informed her.

"What about guns?"

"We are going to pick them up first. My brother-in-law is waiting for us right now," Gonzalez answered, biting the back off of a Cuban cigar and spitting it out of the window.

Semaj continued to look out of the window at the beauty of Cuba. It reminded her of a few parts of Colombia she liked to go to for peace of mind. The countryside looked nice, but things were about to get dark real fast.

Sosa and Mitch walked into the recovery room where Santos was talking to the detective that had been on the scene. He was asking Santos all kinds of questions pertaining to the shooting, but Santos kept his answers simple, he told him that he didn't remember anything that happened before he got shot.

The detective had a feeling that Santos was lying, but there was nothing he could do. He couldn't make him tell the truth and he wasn't going to continue to sit there and repeat the same questions. He just got up and left, passing by Sosa and Mitch on his way out the door.

"How do you feel?" Sosa asked, walking up and standing next to his bed.

"Close the door," he looked over and told Mitch, not wanting the detective that was still standing outside of the room to hear him.

He looked up at Sosa and had a look in his eyes like he wanted to cry. Santos was hurt that he was unable to protect Nyala like he promised Sosa that he would. He felt like he had failed her, so much so that it was hard to look at her.

"I think they're taking her to Jamaica," Santos said, looking away from her in shame.

After Patrick shot Santos, he was still conscious the whole time Patrick was in the house. He just wasn't able to move, but he could hear everything that was going on around him, including some of Patrick's plans to get Nyala out of the States.

"The guy who took her was talking to somebody on the phone. He sounded African or Jamaican," Santos said with a confused look on his face. "He said they were going to meet up at the rest stop somewhere in Florida, right off of I-95."

Santos attempted to sit up in the bed as though he was going after Nyala, but Sosa stopped him. "You was brave and you took a bullet in your chest for my daughter. I'm grateful for that," Sosa said, leaning over and kissing him on the forehead. "I'ma go get her and bring her back. I just want you to get some rest," she continued, rubbing the top of his curly head.

Santos still tried to get out of his bed, but fell backwards in excruciating pain. By the time he opened his eyes, Sosa and Mitch were on their way out of the room. He lay there, clenching his teeth in pain. He wanted to get up so bad and assist Sosa in going to rescue Nyala, but the pain from the bullet wound in his chest wouldn't let him.

Qua drove all the way back to the hotel mad as hell thinking about Ron and the stunt he just tried to pull. He kind of regretted not putting a bullet in his head and felt like because he didn't do it, it was going to come back and bite him in the ass. Ron knew too many intricate details about Qua and how he moved tons of cocaine through the boroughs yearly. If he wanted to, Ron had enough information to put him in prison for the rest of his life.

"Yo, take this car and set it on fire down by the docks," Qua said to one of his boys when he got out of the car in front of the hotel.

He reached into his pocket and pulled out his phone. He looked at it one more time before slamming it to the ground, breaking it into pieces. For insurance purposes, he stomped on what was left of it breaking it into even smaller pieces. He wasn't worried about the contacts in that particular phone because most of them were local drug dealers, people he didn't need to be associated with right now. If the feds were watching like Ron said they were, nobody in that phone was safe.

Qua turned to another one of his boys and asked him about the movement from the Tent members. His boy gave him the rundown telling him that Ezra and his wife went out for dinner while Wong took his men out for a night on the town. Marco and Nikolai stayed in. It wasn't that Nikolai couldn't leave the hotel; it was the fact that she was Marco's responsibility, and he wasn't about to let her skip town on his watch.

"A'ight my nigga. I want you to take some men, go out, and find Ezra and Wong Won. I need eyes on them at all times. Call up to my room the second they get back to the hotel," Qua told his other guard, and then headed into the hotel.

Semaj had a little less than 36 hours to be back with her proof, and although Qua had confidence in Semaj's ability to make shit happen, he knew that if she didn't come back correct, shit was going to get ugly in the city of New York.

Nikolai took a long pull of the cigarette as

she stood by the window looking out into the night sky. She had been in her hotel room for most of the day contemplating her next move. One thing about New York, every ethnic group in the world sought refuge there. The Russians mainly stayed in Manhattan and it didn't take but one phone call to find them. In a matter of hours Nikolai had a nice number of men at her disposal that would pretty much do anything for her because of who she was back in Russia.

"Are you going to go through with this?" Ethan, her top security guard asked from across the room.

He was a little skeptical about the route Nikolai was taking, but nevertheless, he was standing by her.

"I don't think that I have any other choice right now," Nikolai responded, looking out the window.

She felt like her back was up against the wall. It was one thing to be confined to the city limits against her will, but it was another thing to sit there and wait to see whether or not she would live to see another day. As sure as water was wet, if Semaj came to the next meeting with the proof Nikolai tried to kill her, it was a guarantee Nikolai was going to die. Being who she was, Nikolai couldn't swallow that pill and made a choice to bring the whole Tent down with her, starting with Semaj. If she was gonna have to die, everybody was going to have to go. That's just the way she felt and had already set the wheels in motion since that morning.

"It's time we make the city hot like the month of July," Nikolai said, pulling out her cell phone. "You can go now," she said, dismissing Ethan.

She walked back over to the window with the phone to her ear. Nikolai had the pure blood of the devil flowing through her veins and she felt like it was about time for her to show how hard she was willing to go.

"It's nightfall, *Señorita*. I think that it would be safer if we wait until the morning," Gonzalez told Semaj while they sat in the truck a couple of miles away from the Ordoñez's compound.

Semaj looked out of the window at a couple of pedestrians riding past on their bikes. She understood Gonzalez's concerns, but time wasn't on her side. She needed to get the information from Selina and get back to New York as quick as possible. Semaj wasn't even sure if Selina was going to be willing to help her. The last conversation they had, Selina hung up on her and basically told her she was on her own.

"Nah, Gonzalez. We go now. I don't got time for the games. She either gonna help or I'ma make her help."

He could tell by the stone look on Semaj's face that she was dead serious. Gonzalez jumped on his radio to let his men know that it was time to roll out. Two minutes were given so that everyone could check their weapons.

It took about 10 to 15 minutes for Semaj and her convoy to reach the outer walls of the enormous compound. Before their truck could come to a complete stop several Jeeps sped from around the other side of the long wall that wrapped around the compound.

"We got company," Gonzalez yelled through the radio. "Get out of your vehicles," he commanded.

His men exited their trucks—guns hot and ready for confrontation. The two Jeeps that came from out of the compound came to a screeching halt right in front of Semaj's truck. Their headlights were bright, shining their lights on them. Semaj couldn't see that good, but she could hear the doors to one of the Jeeps opening. Two men got out of the red Jeep while two more men stayed in the green Jeep, standing through the roof with M-16s in their possession.

Gonzalez looked back at his men and waved for them to stand down seeing that the men weren't hostile. They all lowered their weapons, but remained on point.

"*¿Cuales son sus negocios aqui?*" the Cuban man asked, standing in front of his Jeep with his rifle pointed at the ground.

"I'm here to speak with Selina," Semaj answered, coming from behind Gonzalez.

"*Salgan de esta tierra o te pegaremos un tiro,*" the man said, threatening to shot at Semaj if she didn't leave.

Semaj was determined and she wasn't gonna just tuck her tail in between her ass and leave. He was gonna have to do a little more than throw threats if he wanted her to leave.

"I'm sorry, but I can't do that," Semaj responded.

A short whistle from the Cuban man is all that was needed for dozens of armed guards to come out of nowhere. They ran from around the wall; both from behind Semaj's men and from behind the Cuban man, all of which had assault rifles aimed at Semaj and her men.

Semaj only had a dozen men with her, but they stood their ground, aiming their weapons back at them. It was a Mexican standoff and neither side budged. Silence filled the air, as the tension got thicker. Gonzalez gripped his AR-15 a little tighter, aiming it at the Cuban man who did all the talking.

"Semaj Espriella!" Selina yelled out, looking down on Semaj and her men who were about to be slaughtered.

Semaj looked up and saw Selina leaning over the top of the wall. She also noticed the ten armed men leaning over the wall with her, pointing their assault rifles directly at her and her men.

"How did I know that you would come," Selina spoke. "All the stories I hear about you, it wasn't hard to predict your next move."

"I'm not here for trouble," Semaj said, waving at her men to lower their weapons in good faith. "I just need you to do one thing for me," she said, reaching in her back pocket and pulling out Raul's cell phone. "All I need is his password," Semaj said, raising the phone up in the air.

Selina looked over at one of her men and nodded for him to go over and get the phone. He did, and then tossed it up to Selina. Semaj thought for a moment that Selina was going to punch the code into the phone, but she didn't. Selina simply looked at the phone, then put it into her back pocket.

"Thank you for returning my brother's property. Now take your men and leave," Selina said, pointing towards the way Semaj and her people came in from.

Semaj felt some type of way about that. She had taken the phone, and dismissed her like she was a peasant. It was very disrespectful and for a split second, Semaj lost it. She reached for the .40 caliber on her waist, but didn't have a chance to pull it out before Gonzalez reached over and grabbed her hand. At the same time, the sound of several guns being cocked filled the air, getting her attention.

"Whoa! Whoa!" Gonzalez yelled out to Selina and her men.

He turned back to face Semaj who still had her hand rested on the butt of her gun. "Semaj, now you know I'll ride with you to the end of the Earth, but I'm asking you to leave this alone. They will slaughter us and we wouldn't stand a chance," Gonzalez told her.

Semaj looked around at the faces of her men and saw that they had no fear. They were willing and ready to die for her; she just didn't want them to die for her in this manner. It took a lot, but Semaj swallowed her pride and did the right thing. She lifted one finger in the air and twirled it in a circle to let her people know to get back in their cars. She glanced up at Selina and gave her a look to say that this wasn't going to be the last time she saw her.

Chapter 9

Patrick drove all night, and by 8:00 in the morning he was in Atlanta, Georgia. Instead of Paulette meeting them in Florida, she decided to wait in Atlanta for them. She didn't want anything to go wrong, plus she couldn't wait to see her niece. She missed going over to Ox's house and seeing Nyala in the living room playing with her toys. She missed taking Nyala out and Ox always telling her that she spoils her too much. After Ox died, she missed her even more because she wasn't able to see her at all.

When Patrick pulled into the motel parking lot, Paulette came outside of her room and walked over to the car. Nyala was still asleep in the back seat. Patrick had an angry look on his face when he got out.

"What's wrong, my love?" Paulette asked, placing both hands on his cheeks and bringing his face down to hers for a kiss.

"She cried herself to sleep," Patrick said, shaking his head.

He had committed all kinds of crimes in Jamaica, including several execution-style murders. This was the first time that he ever had to kidnap a child, and he went against a lot of his morals in doing so. It might sound crazy, but he felt like a monster listening to Nyala cry for her mother while he was driving. He hated to see kids cry and even worse; he hated being the one who made a child cry the way Nyala did.

"I'm sorry you had to do this. I promise that I will make it up to you, my love."

"I'm gonna get a few hours of sleep before we get back on the road," Patrick said. "She been asleep for a couple of hours and I know she should be hungry by now," he informed Paulette before walking off into the motel room.

Paulette opened the back door and grabbed Nyala, cradling her in her arms and taking her into the room. She was a whole lot bigger than the last time she saw her, but nothing could take away the fact that she looked just like Ox and that alone was worth everything she had done to get her back.

"I wanna be back here in time for lunch," Selina told her driver when she got into the back seat of the Lincoln Town Car.

Selina had a lot of errands to run today including picking up Raul's body from the airport. The State of New York finally sent his remains after they conducted a full autopsy and investigation. Selina was going to have a proper burial for him tomorrow, right next to Julio, their other brother who died at the hands of Valentina, Semaj's grandmother.

"Come on! Come on!" Selina said, snapping her fingers at the driver.

When the tall double doors opened up, Semaj was sitting on a bench right in front of the compound. She appeared to be alone, but Gonzalez wasn't that far up the road. Semaj just wanted to talk to Selina one on one without any of the manly testosterones floating around.

"Stop the car," Selina told her driver, seeing Semaj standing there by herself.

She got out of the car and when some of her guards came from out of the compound to assist her, she waived them off. She even made them close the doors to the compound behind them.

"You people are crazy in the States," Selina said, shaking her head as she crossed the little dirt road to get over to Semaj. "What do you want from me?" she asked, walking over and taking a seat on the bench.

Semaj thought that coming with a more

humbled attitude would get her better results and it seemed to be working.

"The same crazy bitch that killed your brother has been trying to kill me. The Tent gave me 48 hours to prove it or be removed as a member. Your brother had a recorded conversation with him and Nikolai plotting to assassinate me," Semaj explained.

"Give me one reason why I should help you," Selina said, looking over at Semaj.

Semaj sat there and thought about it. She could only think of one reason that made any sense.

"Our families have a long history together and I think that it's time we move forward instead of living off the old mistakes they made. We are the new leaders of our families and right now we have the opportunity to stop any further animosity between us," Semaj said sincerely.

Selina put her head down and smiled. She actually did like the sound of squashing the beef between their families since it never benefitted anybody. The killings and shootings were only going to lead up to more unnecessary bloodshed. At some point it had to end.

"One thing about you city girls, y'all sure do have a pocket full of slick talk," Selina joked, reaching into her pants pocket and pulling out Raul's phone.

Selina punched in his four-digit pin number, and then passed the phone to Semaj. She grabbed it and put it to her ear with a big smile on her face. That smile quickly turned into a frown once she heard Nikolai and Raul talking about killing her. The conversation was raw and uncut, and Semaj couldn't believe the lack of regard they had for her life. They talked like Semaj was a worthless piece of trash thrown out on the street.

"I think that's your people," Selina said, pointing down the road at an oncoming vehicle speeding their way.

As the car got closer Selina could see that there were two of them. She looked down the road in the opposite direction and saw another vehicle kicking up dirt, driving at high speeds coming their way. Semaj looked too, but she didn't notice the cars. Surely they weren't from her convoy. She looked the other way and saw the other cars coming in the opposite direction. They, too, were unfamiliar to her.

"Those aren't my people," Semaj said, bringing the phone down from her ear and putting in into her back pocket.

When the cars got within 25 yards of the front doors to the compound, Semaj felt that something was wrong. There were even more cars than they had originally thought.

"Come on, Selina," Semaj said, grabbing her by the arm and pulling her across the road.

Semaj drew her .40 cal once the first Bronco

came to a stop not that far away from her. It was a good thing she did because the men who were in the truck jumped out and started letting bullets fly. Da, Da, Da, Da, Da, Da, Da! La, La, La, La, La!

Semaj released a couple led balls herself, sending them right at the gunmen and the Bronco they pulled up in.

"Open the door!" Selina yelled, looking over her shoulders at the other vehicles pulling up.

Semaj let it rip. She had ten shots in her .40 cal and let off four, followed by another four, striking one of the gunmen in his chest. Selina's driver rolled out of the Town Car in the nick of time as bullets tore through the front windshield.

As the other trucks pulled up, the tall doors to the compound opened up slightly to allow Selina and Semaj inside. Selina's driver wasn't as fortunate. He was hit several times in the back before he could reach the door. His body dropped right at the entrance as the doors were closing.

"Who in the fuck was that?" Semaj asked, running side by side next to Selina, into the main house.

"I don't know. I've never seen them before."

Right after Selina responded, her security went into combat mode. They rushed the walls of the compound firing down on the unknown gunmen. Other parts of her security team sped out the back of the compound to engage the shooters on the outside. Within seconds a vicious gun battle ensued.

"We gotta get out of here," Semaj said, watching as personnel ran through the house to get outside.

"No, we're safe here," Selina said, walking down the narrow hallway in the middle of the house.

She had a lot of confidence in her security team and felt that the confrontation wasn't going to last long at all. Semaj, on the other hand, had a gut instinct that told her Nikolai had something to do with this. If that was the case, the gun battle was going to be a lot worse than what Selina expected.

"Selina, I need you to trust me. If the people outside of those walls are who I think they are, we're as good as dead if we stay in this house," Semaj said, pulling out her cell phone. She called Gonzalez who wasn't that far up the road and told him the situation. There was only one way he would respond and that was to come in hot.

Kaboooooomm! Kaboooomm! Kabooooommm!

Three loud blasts rocked the entire house causing Semaj and Selina to get low and cover their ears. Selina had the fear of God in her eyes after hearing that. It was getting real.

"I have to get my mother," Selina said, stumbling down the hallway towards her mother's room.

Semaj ran behind her with Gonzalez still on the other end of the phone. She informed him to come in through the back way instead of the front to avoid the serious gun battle.

Semaj could hear guns being fired inside of the main house and knew that the men had stormed the compound. Yelling could also be heard, but Semaj couldn't make out the language.

"Let's go!" Semaj yelled at Selina who was bringing her mother out of one of the rooms.

Just as they were heading down the hallway towards the back, a man with an assault rifle ran down the hallway shooting into the ceiling as if he was trying to get them to stop running. Semaj quickly raised her gun up and fired her last two shots at him, hitting him in his chest and stomach.

When they got out back, Gonzalez and his men pulled up and jumped out. Semaj, Selina, and Selina's mother ran across the backyard to get to the trucks. Semaj made it to the trucks first, jumping inside. Selina fell to the ground trying to help her mother.

First it was loud yelling and then two gunmen appeared from out of the back door to the house. They began shooting wildly at the trucks. Gonzalez was two seconds away from leaving Selina and her mother, but Semaj wasn't having it. Flashbacks of them leaving Sosa behind crossed her mind and she wasn't about to let that happen again on her watch.

She grabbed a mini 14 from inside of the truck she was in, got out, and began firing at the two men. They dipped and took cover back inside of the house, giving Selina and her mother enough time to get to the trucks. In a matter of seconds, Gonzalez and his men sped away from the compound with everybody alive.

Nyala opened her eyes and sat up on the bed. She looked around and didn't see anybody, but smelled the heavy scent of McDonald's in the air. It only made her hungrier then what she already was. She looked over and saw the bag of food on the table, but was too scared to get off the bed. The voice of a woman startled her and when she turned around, Paulette was coming out of the bathroom.

"Hi, Ny Ny," Paulette greeted her in a soft tone and with a big smile on her face when she walked over to the bed.

Nyala had a confused look on her face at first, but then remembered who Paulette was. She managed to crack a smile and crawl over to the other side of the bed and give her a hug. This was the first familiar face she had seen since Patrick walked her past Santos's dead body on their way out the door. To see Paulette made her feel like she was safe.

"Aunt P, I wanna go home," Nyala said, holding on to her.

Paulette hugged her back, happy to finally get her back. It's been a long time coming and Paulette didn't have any plans on letting Nyala out of her sight.

"Auntie P gotta tell you something," Paulette said, ready to tell her biggest lie yet. "That bad man who came and took you, he killed ya mommy. She's in heaven now," Paulette said, with a straight face.

Nyala began to cry, and Paulette consoled her like the good aunt she wanted Nyala to think she was. As she was holding onto her, Patrick came walking through the door. Paulette quickly gave him a look and a nod to let him know to leave before she saw him. He did, right before Nyala turned her head and looked towards the door. They sat there and held each other for a while until Nyala stopped crying. It was hard to do, but very necessary if Paulette wanted Nyala to accept her as her new guardian. With Sosa out of the way more than likely, Nyala would look to her aunt for each and everything and that's just the way Paulette wanted it to be.

Chapter **10**

Semaj looked out of the windows at the clouds that passed by the G-4 jet as they traveled back to New York from Cuba. Semaj brought Selina and her mother back with them, so that they would be protected.

"They killed many of my people and they burned my house to the ground," Selina told Semaj, as she took a seat across from her. "I don't understand who would want to do something like this."

Semaj knew exactly who was behind it. At first she couldn't figure out the language the shooters were speaking when they attacked the compound, but at the end, right before the two men came out of the house from the back door, Semaj heard them speaking in Russian. Semaj couldn't speak Russian at all, but she did learn a couple of words when she visited the country last summer on business. The words "stop" and "kill" were a few she remembered, so when she heard the men use those two words, Semaj knew that they had to be Russian.

"Nikolai just tried to kill you," Semaj looked over and told her.

"What? What do you mean?" Selina questioned her, with a baffled expression on her face. "I don't even know Nikolai like that."

"She must have known I was going to come to you for help," Semaj explained.

The more Selina thought about it, the more it made sense to her. Nikolai was vicious and now she saw firsthand how ugly it could get. Nobody was exempt, not even members of the Tent. It was time to expose Nikolai and put her right where she needed to be, and that was six feet under the ground.

Nyala sat on the bed staring at the TV while Paulette packed the rest of the items she was taking with them on the road. It was still early in the afternoon, but Paulette figured she'd get a jump on the traffic especially since she would be doing all the driving down to Florida, being that she couldn't be seen with Patrick by Nyala. He was the bad man who took her away and killed her mother, as far as she was convinced. But Paulette had a little trick up her sleeve for that, too.

"It's me! It's me!" Nyala yelled, pointing at the

TV. "Aunt P, look," she continued.

Paulette turned around to see Nyala's face all over the news. She almost had a heart attack looking at the screen. An Amber alert was issued in Atlanta along with other major cities from Brooklyn to Miami. The mass exposure came from the many connections Sosa had up and down the East Coast.

"Shit!" Paulette mumbled under her breath. "Nyala why don't you watch some cartoons while Auntie P go get us something to drink from the vending machines." She smiled, changing the channel before Sosa's face came popping up on the screen next.

Due to the change in sleeping arrangements, Patrick had to get another room a few doors down in order to stay away from Nyala. Paulette had a key so it wasn't anything for her to barge into the room while he was still asleep. The door slamming woke him up.

"She's on the Amber alert. Her face is all over the TV," Paulette said, turning on his TV. She walked over and took a seat on the bed next to him. The news went to commercial, but Patrick slid to the edge of the bed to listen to her.

"I need you to do something important for me," she said in her most soft and innocent voice.

Patrick knew that Paulette wanted something big. Anytime she spoke in this manner, there was always a catch to what she wanted and today wasn't any different.

"You have to go back and kill Sosa," she said, leaning over and resting her head on his shoulders. "As long as she's alive, she's gonna come for her."

"Come on, Paulette. We're already gone. Me don't want ta go back," Patrick complained.

Paulette wasn't trying to hear it. She knew she had Patrick right where she wanted and just a little more incentive would push him over the edge. She reached up and kissed him on the neck.

"Don't you wanna make me happy?" she said, getting up and straddling him on the bed. "I promise I won't ask you to do anything like dis again," she said, pushing him back onto the bed.

"Yeah, right." He laughed, knowing that was a lie.

She began kissing him on his lips, then down the center of his bare chest. Patrick put his hand on top of her head and pushed it down further towards his dick. Paulette didn't resist. In fact, she encouraged it, grabbing his pants by the waist and pulling them down by his thighs. His soft dick sagged to the right and all it took was a few kisses for it to wake up. He was fully erect within seconds and in one swift gulp, Paulette devoured the whole of his member.

"Blood clot," Patrick moaned, looking down at Paulette's thick, full, juicy lips going up and down on his dick.

In a matter of minutes, Patrick gave into her warm, wet, and soft mouth. He tried to pull her head off his dick so he wouldn't cum in her mouth, but Paulette insisted on it, knocking his hand away. That alone made him want to cum inside of her mouth, and he did, splashing off like a super soaker.

Paulette continued to suck and swallow every drop of his thick, warm cum, causing Patrick to clinch his ass cheeks together. She looked up at him and the pleasure he had written all over his face assured Paulette that Patrick was gonna do just about anything she asked him to do. Sosa was pretty much good as dead, and hopefully, if everything panned out the way Paulette wanted it to, Patrick would be dead right along with her.

As soon as the jet landed, Semaj jumped on the phone to call Qua and let him know that she was back. He didn't answer the phone the first try, but Semaj called back and he answered on the second ring.

"Yooo," he answered in a groggy voice.

"What are you doin'?" She smiled, happy to hear his voice.

"I was asleep. I been up all night tryin' to keep track of everybody's movement," Qua said, sitting up in the bed. "What about you? Did you make out okay?"

Semaj explained everything that went on in
Cuba and how she believed Nikolai was behind the
attempted murder on Selina's life. It didn't surprise
Qua one bit though. He knew how sick the crazy
Russian broad could be. The good news was,
Semaj made it back to the States with the proof
she needed. The bad news was, they had other
problems to deal with, too.

"Yo, I didn't want to bother you wit' da bullshit
right now, but it's important," Qua said, getting up
and walking to the bathroom.

"Talk to me."

"The feds is watching me. I don't know how
long it's been goin' on for, but you was right about
da nigga Ron that was wit' me that day. He was
wearing a wire. I got rid of my other phone and
all," he told her.

Qua explained the events that went on
the night before with Ron and how he felt that
somebody had been following behind him most of
the night. He also told her about the feds trying to
take Sosa down and how they were using Ron to
set her up. Semaj just sat there and listened to him.

"So look, once you take care of the situation
with Nikolai, I'ma fall back for a while. If they
watchin' me I'm not gonna bring them around you."

"I get it, but listen; I need you to do
something for me. I gotta put Selina and her mom
up somewhere safe. While I'm doing that, I need

for you to get the families together for a meeting tonight. We can have it back at the warehouse around 9 o'clock."

"It's done. I'll call you once everything is confirmed," Qua responded, walking back into the room. "Oh, and be careful," he warned in a concerned tone.

"I will babe; and Quasim, I love you," she said, before hanging up the phone.

Both Qua and Semaj looked at the phone. It's been a long time since Semaj used words like "babe" or "love" when it came to Qua. To hear her say that she loved him, Qua couldn't stop smiling. Semaj couldn't believe she even said it. She just got caught up in the moment and that probably came from her thinking about him more than usual lately. Whatever it was, she was beginning to find it hard to conceal the true feelings she had bottled up for Qua and the next time the opportunity presented itself, she was gonna let him know exactly how she felt.

As soon as Semaj got off the phone with Qua, she decided to check up on Sosa and to let her know that she was back in the city. She had no idea what Sosa was going through right now, but as soon as Sosa answered the phone, Semaj knew something was wrong.

"You back?" Sosa asked, wiping the tears from her face.

"Yeah, what's wrong?"

Sosa was losing her mind about Nyala being kidnapped. She really didn't know how to explain the situation since it happened so fast. The only thing she knew is that Ox's people were behind it. Who it was, was still a mystery to her.

"Where are you?" Semaj asked, after hearing Sosa break everything down to her.

"I'm at Santos's house. Your dad here wit' me so I'm straight. I just gotta sit here and think for a minute," Sosa said, looking down at the blood stained carpet where Santos was shot.

"A'ight, don't move. I'll be there in 30 minutes," Semaj said, before hanging up the phone.

Semaj leaned up against the passenger door of the truck shaking her head. If it wasn't one thing it was another, and as she stood there looking into the sky at the planes passing by, she wondered if all the drama in her life was ever going to end. At one point, she felt like just giving up and leaving the life of crime alone for good, but the only thing stopping her was that she was in too deep. If she had quit now, too many loose ends would be untied, and just like karma, it would fall back on her eventually, leaving her in the same position she was when she bowed out.

Santos sat up in his bed in pain, lightly placing his hand over his chest where the bullet had been lodged. A combination of morphine and the ambition to find Nyala, gave him enough strength to move around a bit.

"Whoa! Whoa!" one of Mitch's guards said, walking into the room. "Just let me know what you need and I'll have the nurse bring it to you," the man said.

Both of Santos's feet were on the ground and he didn't have any plans of putting them back in the bed. "Yo, what's yo' name son?" Santos asked, looking over at the man.

"I'm CJ. I work for Mitch. He told me to stay wit' you and make sure you was alright," he answered.

Santos looked around the room again, this time trying to fully stand on his feet. He fell back down on the bed once his legs told him that he wasn't ready to walk. Santos was determined though. He tried again, but still had no luck, prompting CJ to run over and try to stop him.

"Come on, yo. Just cool out," CJ tried to advise.

"CJ, I want you to listen to me clearly. I gotta get da fuck out of this hospital. You either gon' help me or back da fuck up," Santos snapped.

CJ saw conviction in his eyes when he spoke and knew that no matter what, Santos was out of there. He didn't want to be the one Mitch snapped on if something was to happen to him after he left the hospital so instead of backing da fuck up like Santos said, CJ stepped up and assisted him in his great escape.

Chapter 11

"I just got the call. Semaj is back in the city and she called a meeting," Marco said, taking a seat next to Nikolai at the bar. "I'm guessing she found whatever it was she was looking for," Marco continued, waving for the bartender to come over and take his order.

Nikolai threw back another shot of scotch, her fifth since she'd been sitting there. After she got the call from her people in Cuba telling her Selina and Semaj managed to get away, she figured Semaj got the proof she needed.

"Do you know what happens when you apply pressure to pipes that are already at the brink of blowing?" Nikolai said, cutting her eyes over at him.

Marco waited for the bartender to pour his and Nikolai's shot of scotch. When he walked off, Marco answered her. "I guess you'll have a bloody mess to clean up," he said, throwing back his shot.

Nikolai had her back up against the wall and the only way she knew how to come up out of her situation was by violence. That's the only thing people really respect these days and for anybody in the Tent who thought that they were going to just kill Nikolai without her putting up a fight, they were sadly mistaken.

"If you were smart, and I know you are, it would be wise of you to leave tonight, because if you're still here when the shit hits the fan, it's going to get all over you," Nikolai warned, throwing back her last and final shot of scotch.

She got up from the bar, put her jacket on and walked off. Marco took in a deep breath, and then exhaled in frustration. It was beyond a shadow of a doubt that Nikolai was about to turn the fire up another notch under the Tent, and Marco knew her so well that he actually considered her advice about leaving tonight. One thing about her was that she didn't have any picks when it came down to her murder game, and Marco of all people knew firsthand the pain she was capable of inflicting on her enemies.

Semaj pulled into Santos's driveway damn near running into the garage door with the Tahoe. Mitch was standing at the front door waiting for her. "I got a call that you called a Tent meeting tonight?"

Mitch asked, hugging Semaj when she got up the steps.

"Yeah Daddy, but I don't know if I'm gonna make it. Is Sosa in there?" Semaj asked, walking past him.

"Yeah, she's here. But what do you mean you might not make it," he said, following behind her.

Sosa was sitting in the kitchen rolling up some Sour Diesel at the table. She hadn't smoked weed in years, but couldn't think of anything else that would calm her nerves down right now. She didn't know what to think about the abduction and it scared the hell out of her to think that she might not ever see Nyala again.

"You don't need this," Semaj said, walking into the kitchen and grabbing the Dutch out of Sosa's hand right before she was about to light it. "Come 'er," she said, wrapping her arms around Sosa.

She gave Sosa the hug that she needed right now and she broke down crying. Semaj was her best friend and Sosa, although older, looked up to her like a big sister.

"First priority is to get her back," Semaj said aloud for Sosa and Mitch to hear.

When it came to family, everything else got put on hold until the issue was resolved. That's just the way Semaj was schooled and Mitch couldn't even argue with her, not that he wanted to.

"Is it Ox's people?" Semaj knew the history of the Jamaicans and how they roll.

"Yeah, I'm sure of it," Sosa said, nodding her head.

"I just don't have a clue of who though and where they're taking my baby," she said, as she began to cry.

Before Semaj could say anything, Sosa's phone started ringing in the other room. Remembering Penny was supposed to be taking care of some running around for her, Sosa got up from the table to go answer it. Normally, Sosa ignored blocked numbers, but with Nyala missing, all calls were getting answered.

"Hello."

"I haven't heard this voice in a very long time," Paulette spoke into the phone. "Do you know who this is?" she asked, in her deep Jamaican accent.

Sosa's heart dropped down into her stomach. She never forgets a face or a voice and since she knew Paulette well, it wasn't hard to figure out who she was.

"Paulette?" Sosa asked, just to be sure.

"Ahhhh, you got it, mom. Look, me gon' tell you one time and one time only—"

"Where is my daughter, Paulette?" she asked, cutting Paulette off before she could finish her sentence. Sosa walked all the way outside so that Semaj and Mitch couldn't hear her conversation.

"Nyala's fine, Sosa. She's with her family now."

"I am her family, Paulette!"

If she could, Sosa would have reached through the phone and grabbed Paulette by the throat. She should have known that if somebody in Ox's family was capable of doing something like this, it would have been Paulette.

"Here's what's going to happen. You are not going to try and find us and you will tell the police you found Nyala with a family member and she's safe. You do as I ask and I will let you see Nyala when she turns 18," Paulette said.

Sosa became furious listening to Paulette's demands. She had to take the phone away from her face in order to get her thoughts together. There was no way in hell Sosa was going to comply with anything Paulette said, and she was going to make that known.

"Paulette, I swear on my little girl's life that I am going to spend every dollar I got and every second of my time finding you. And when I finally catch you... and I don't care how long it takes, I'm going to kill you with my bare hands," Sosa said, and then hung up the phone.

Paulette twisted her face up looking down at her phone in disbelief that Sosa made her threat then hung up. Paulette's heart began racing fast from fear that Sosa was going to stand on what she said. She knew that Sosa meant every word and with her money, power, and respect she had all over, there wasn't a place on earth Paulette could hide, especially in Jamaica. She had expected all of this and that's why Patrick was on his way back to New York to put Sosa in a body bag, just so Paulette wouldn't have to worry about looking over her shoulders for the rest of her life. Even still, just hearing Sosa say those words sent chills down Paulette's spine.

Being labeled as a rat in the hood was similar to a child molester living next door to an elementary school. Everybody hated him, nobody wanted to talk to him, and somebody always wanted to kill him. That was the treatment Ron was getting from the hood after Qua put it out in the streets he was working for the police. Wasn't anybody trying to mess with him. He couldn't even buy a bag of weed in the city.

"You ready to tally up?" the bartender asked, walking over to Ron who had found himself drinking his problems away in a bar in downtown Manhattan.

This was the only place that would accept his money anyway. Qua really made it hard for him to do anything and that included making money as well. Ron wasn't broke, but he definitely wasn't in the position financially that he never had to hustle or work again. Eventually, the bread that he did have was going to run out and if that happened, he didn't know what he was going to do. All he knew was New York and he never could see himself living anywhere else, but at this point it didn't look good for him.

There was only one person in this world that had the power to reverse everything that was happening to him. Just as easy as it was for Qua to give the word for niggas to stop messing with Ron, he could easily go back and re-stamp him as being official. Qua had the authority to do that, but more than likely he wasn't going to. Ron would have to do something so big and so gangsta that the hood couldn't deny him a G-pass. Something so huge that even Qua would have to tilt his hat to him, and as Ron threw back shot after shot of Ciroc, his brain started pondering.

A couple of hours had passed by and Semaj continued to stay by Sosa's side, waiting for her to make a move. Whatever Sosa wanted to do, Semaj was going to back her play no matter what. If Sosa decided she was going to go to war with Jamaica, Semaj was going to call in the troops. That's just how she was when it came down to family.

"Hold on, let me take this," Mitch said, looking down at his phone.

Semaj and Sosa remained at the kitchen table in silence, both thinking about Nyala. Mitch came right back in the kitchen to inform them on what was going on with the Tent.

"They wanna know if we're still coming," Mitch said, tucking his phone back in his jacket pocket.

The Tent meeting officially started 15 minutes ago and everybody was there except Semaj, Sosa, and Mitch. If they weren't going to make it, Nikolai was going to be free to leave and Semaj would no longer be a member of the Tent indefinitely.

"Yeah, y'all should go," Sosa suggested.

"I'm not leaving you," Semaj responded. "Fuck the Tent, they can't survive without me anyway."

"Semaj, you gotta deal with this," Mitch chimed in.

"Yeah Maj, you can't let Nikolai win like that. She's gonna keep coming after you until she kills you. You got a chance to finish this, so go take care of that real quick and come back when it's over. I'ma be sitting right here," Sosa assured her.

"Yeah and I'll leave Blue and Trey here to watch the house," Mitch said.

As much as Semaj hated to admit it, Sosa was right about Nikolai. It's been going on long enough and it was about time to put an end to the drama before Nikolai became successful in actually killing Semaj. With the proof that Semaj had, it wouldn't take that long for the members of the Tent to find her guilty and sentence her to death.

"I'll go to the Tent meeting only if you promise me that you won't do anything until I get back," Semaj said to Sosa.

Sosa smiled and agreed. Wasn't nothing going to happen in the next couple of hours anyway or at least that's what she wanted Semaj to think. The whole time Sosa and Semaj sat there in silence, Sosa had put together a plan in finding out where Nyala was. All she really had to do was get everybody out of the house and wait patiently for things to fall in line.

Chapter 12

An all black Tahoe crept into the warehouse where the awaiting Tent members sat talking amongst themselves at the table. A second black Tahoe pulled in right behind the first one, and simultaneously all eight doors opened up, and out jumped Semaj and her people. On her way to the meeting she stopped by and picked up Selina, in order for her to bring even more clarity to the situation.

Semaj and her people looked like they came fresh out of the military the way they were dressed. Semaj had on a pair of green cargo army pants, an all black t-shirt and a pair of tan 3.5 inch Timberland boots. She looked like she was ready for war and so was her security who were wearing the same thing, except that they had MP5 machine guns clutched in their hands.

"Sosa won't be able to make it tonight. She's dealing with family issues," Semaj said walking up to the table, pulling out a Glock 9mm and taking a seat at the head of the table.

She sat the gun on the table right in front of her then sat up in her chair like the boss that she was. Everyone was silent, waiting for Semaj to get down to business. She looked around at everybody who was looking back at her. For a moment, she wanted to jump over the table and smack the smirk off Nikolai's face. Knowing that her time was officially up kept Semaj calm and relaxed.

"So do you have it? Do you have proof that Nikolai tried to kill you," Marco asked as he became tired of Semaj's dramatic approach.

Semaj looked at him then reached into her cargo pocket and grabbed Raul's phone. She looked into the screen and pressed a few buttons. Moments later the voices of Nikolai and Raul appeared. Everybody at the table sat and listened attentively.

"I see Marco's not too enthused about the whole situation. Are you sure we can trust that he won't say anything?

"Marco's backing out. He really doesn't want to be involved with it, but he did give me his word that he would never speak of it to anybody."

Everyone at the table shifted their eyes over at Marco, who was sitting there sweating under his arms. Shocked to know that he had something to do with it initially, Ezra just shook his head. The recording continued though.

"Do you need any help with this?" he questioned.

"No, my people in Colombia are taking care of everything as we speak. My men are good at what they do," Nikolai assured him.

"Good, because Semaj has to go. Her family is taking over the whole damn Tent. The longer she stays alive, the more all of our seats are in jeopardy," he stated.

That was the end of the recording and everybody at the table sat in silence. Semaj looked over at Nikolai. The grin she had had on her face had disappeared and was replaced by a frown. She honestly didn't think that Semaj would get the proof she needed, and if she did, Nikolai damn sure didn't think that she was gonna make it out of Cuba alive.

Wong Won wiped over his face before reaching into his waist and pulling his gun out. Ezra did the same thing, resting his gun on the table, but pointed at Nikolai. Semaj's gun was already out; all she did was take the safety off and point it at Nikolai. Mitch pulled his pistol, too, and so did Selina. Nikolai's men backed off of her, wanting to avoid being hit by one of the many bullets that was about to come her way. The crazy part about it, Nikolai didn't break a sweat looking around at all of the guns. She sat up in her chair and interlocked her fingers on top of the table.

"Apologize to Semaj and we will make it swift. One bullet, no pain, open casket," Wong Won offered.

"You're not gonna kill me." Nikolai chuckled, looking Wong directly in his eyes.

"And what makes you think that? Look around, Nikolai. It's over for you," Wong responded.

Nikolai shook her head. While everybody from the Tent was out running around all night, she was putting in work from the comfort of her hotel room. She wasn't gonna go out like this, not if she could help it, anyway. What came out of her mouth next was enough to catch everybody's attention.

"Wong, you have a daughter, Maylee, she attends NYU. I believe she's studying medicine," she said, sitting back in her chair. "I have men at her dorm right now that won't hesitate putting a bullet in her head the second she opens her door. Ezra..." She smiled, turning her attention to him. "Why would you leave your wife in the hotel, and bring just about every last one of your security guards here with you?" she said, nodding over his shoulder at his assassins lined up against the wall. "Mitch, don't think for one second that I don't know Semaj stashed a little over a ton of cocaine inside your condo. One phone call from my people and you'll see what the federal penitentiary looks like on the inside... Marco, they were about to kill you, too, so consider this a favor," she said without even cutting her eyes over at him. "You'll be leaving with me tonight... And we have Semaj, the boss of all bosses. The reason why Sosa couldn't make it here tonight was because her daughter, Nyala, was kidnapped. My men were there and saw the whole abduction unfold. They know that Sosa is sitting in the house right now with two of Mitch's watchdogs looking over her. I'll have her killed before she has the chance to save her little girl," Nikolai threatened.

"Urrrgggg," Semaj grunted, getting up from her seat.

She walked over to Nikolai and pressed the nose of her gun up against her forehead. She wanted to pull the trigger so bad, but she couldn't. Too much was at stake. Too many lives were in jeopardy. Semaj lowered her weapon in frustration and so did everybody else at the table.

"When I leave this warehouse, my men will leave your people," Nikolai said, rising to her feet.

She looked around the room to see if anybody had any objections, which they didn't. Everyone knew Nikolai well enough to know that she wasn't bluffing. She had them right where she wanted and didn't one soul sitting at the table stop her and her men from walking out of the warehouse with Marco tailing behind. The moment she did leave, everyone pulled out their phones to call and check up on their people.

"Now what do we have here," Agent Davis said, looking through his binoculars at the front door of the warehouse. "They got Benzs, BMWs, Range Rovers, and Tahoes up in there. Make sure you take pictures of everybody that comes walking out that door," Davis told Mason.

They had Semaj under surveillance the moment her jet landed in New York. After careful thought, Davis had come to the conclusion and was under the impression that Semaj may have been Sosa. Everything added up, especially her connection to the Milano family.

"I need license plate numbers, too," Davis said, watching as the members of the Tent poured out of the warehouse and got into their cars. "I think it's time we go to the boss with this. We're gonna need some more manpower," he said, his binoculars glued to the front windshield.

Davis could tell from the luxury cars and serious faces that this was some kind of meeting and not just a casual get-together. Something huge was going on and he could feel it in the air. Davis was something like a bloodhound; when he got a scent on criminal activities being conducted, he would lock in until he found what he was looking for.

"Yo man, I don't think you should have left the hospital," CJ looked over and told Santos while he was driving. "Just let me call Mitch."

"Man, put the phone down," Santos barked as he adjusted his arm in his sling.

Santos felt responsible for Nyala being kidnapped. He beat himself up for not being on point, even though there wasn't much that he could do about Patrick sneaking up on him in the house. It could have happened to anybody, even Sosa, but it didn't and that was a tough pill for Santos to swallow.

"Pull over right here," he directed CJ, pointing to a small apartment complex.

"Who live here?"

"Stop asking so many questions."

Santos wasn't strong enough to do any walking and since he made a phone call right before he left the hospital, he didn't have to. It only took about a minute for a tall, dark-skinned man to appear from the building. He had a book bag in his hand and his fitted hat was cocked low over his eyes.

"Roll my window down," Santos told CJ as the man approached the vehicle.

"Yo, what up Corey. You look good," Santos greeted with a nod of his head.

"Damn my nigga. You wasn't lying when you said you got hit," Corey responded, looking at Santos's arm in a sling. "Everything you need is in the bag."

It wasn't that long ago Santos was knee deep in the game. His name use to ring bells all throughout the Bronx, and he was known for three things: getting money, fuckin' bitches, and squeezing that trigger. It took his little brother getting murdered right in front of his face, for him to want to leave the game alone. He did leave the game, too, but he never forgot where he came from, nor did he forget what a gun looked like.

"How's mom dukes?" Santos asked Corey as he passed the book bag over to CJ.

"She good. You know she somewhere blowin' some tree right now." Corey chuckled. "But look, if you need me, I can hop in da back seat right now," he said with a serious look on his face.

"Nah homie, I'm good. I already got one co-defendant and you know that's one too many."

Corey smiled, agreeing with him in that aspect. He should have known better than to ask that kind of question. Santos was the type to do his dirt all by his lonely. Today wasn't any different, and CJ better pray that he don't show one sign of weakness because if he does, Santos won't hesitate leaving his body stinking as well.

"Did you call?" Nikolai looked over and asked Marco as they sat in the back seat of Marco's Range.

"Yeah, the wheels go up as soon as we get there," Marco replied. "Do you actually think they're going to let us live? They are gonna hunt us down and kill us no matter where we go," he told her, thinking about what he'd do if he was in their shoes.

Nikolai violated the Tent to a degree that the only punishment for her actions was death. Everything would be put on hold and nothing was gonna move until she was dead. It was either she died, or a war would be waged against her people by every single member of the Tent.

"You can come back to Russia with me if you are scared. I'm sure I can find something for you to do," Nikolai joked in a teasingly, seductive voice.

"You think that this is a game? You really don't think that these people are capable of...."

"Capable of what!" Nikolai shouted back at him. "I know they will come for me, but what else can I do? I'll just have to deal with that when it happens."

Marco was on some other shit right now. He was never big on running away from his problems and he wasn't afraid to get his hands dirty a little bit. He definitely knew that the Tent wasn't going to let him live for his part in the assassination attempt. He felt he only had one option.

"I say we stay and fight," Marco said, looking Nikolai right in her eyes. "Let's stay and fight until every last one of them is dead."

"Are you serious?"

"I got plenty of guns here and a nice number of men on standby ready to move."

Marco knew that this was the only thing that they could do at this point if they wanted to live. One of the many good things about the city and state of New York, just about every nationality in the world lived there. It wasn't anything for Marco to round up some extra men and put guns in their hands. Nikolai also had a nice-sized Russian community she could lean on for some support.

"Driver! Turn the car around," Nikolai instructed, tapping him on his shoulder. "You say we stay and fight, then we stay and fight," she said, looking over at him.

Chapter 13

Not one light was on downstairs, and the only reason why Sosa was capable of seeing was from the upstairs hallway light shining down the steps. That's all the light Sosa really needed considering her reasons for sitting in the dark, on the floor and in the corner of the living room. She jammed herself between the love sofa and the wall.

"Damn!" she whispered, rubbing her numb legs.

She had been sitting back there for hours, thinking that her threats to Paulette would make her come back and try to eliminate her from the equation completely. Sosa knew Jamaicans well enough to know how arrogant and cocky they were, especially Ox's family, who believed they needed to be in control of every situation, and Sosa banked on Paulette feeling the same way.

"She's not coming back," Sosa sulked, ready to get up and stretch her legs.

As soon as she was about to get up a clicking noise came from the direction of the basement. It was so quiet in the house, Sosa could hear very light footsteps coming up the basement stairs. For a second, she couldn't believe Paulette actually came back, but she was grateful and anxious to greet her.

"Bring that ass on," Sosa whispered to herself, looking into the dining room where the basement door was.

At first it was just a shadow, but then, as they came closer, Sosa could see that it was a man. He was tall and black with a large gun in his hand. Sosa's heart started racing at the sight of him and knew that he was there to kill her and probably anyone who was in the house.

He slowly crept to the bottom of the steps, and for the first time Sosa could see his face. She didn't know who Patrick was, but by the looks of his dreads draping down over his shoulders, she knew that he was Jamaican. He stood at the bottom of the steps looking up and listening for any sounds of movement.

Sosa tried to get up, but her legs had completely gone to sleep on her, making it difficult to move. She was only about 12 feet away from him, but couldn't move. It was frustrating, but Sosa wasn't going to let her chance miss her. She raised the Glock .40 and turned the infrared beam on, aiming it to the back of his head. He was about to go up the steps, but Sosa stopped him.

"Take another step and I'ma open the back of ya head up," Sosa threatened.

Patrick froze. He knew the voice was coming from behind him, but he didn't know from where. He was sure he didn't see anybody when he emerged from the basement, but even he was capable of slipping.

"Drop the gun," Sosa demanded as she slowly began to come from behind the loveseat.

Patrick didn't do it. He only gripped his gun tighter, and was two seconds away from turning around and letting it fly. He didn't comply so Sosa aimed the beam down at his hand. She fired a single shot. Pow! The bullet hit him in his wrist bone forcing him to drop the gun anyway.

"Urrrrggggg!" he yelled, grabbing his wrist.

He went to go pick up the gun, but Sosa was all over him. She had regained enough feeling in her legs to run over and grab the gun off the floor before he could. She backed up with both guns in her hand until she got to the light switch. Patrick stood there in pain while Sosa shined some light on the situation.

"Get down on the ground!" Sosa belted, seeing his face for the very first time.

"Fuck you. Shoot me," Patrick shot back.

Sosa didn't think twice. She pulled the trigger again, this time shooting him in his kneecap. He fell back on the steps yelling in pain. He grabbed his knee, but his hand was still bleeding. He didn't know what to do.

"Blood clot, bitch," Patrick yelled out, looking over at Sosa holding the two guns on him.

Sosa walked over to him, stuffing his gun into her waist while still holding the Glock. She grabbed a handful of his dreads and pulled him to the floor. She wasn't playing any games with him at all and wanted to get straight down to the business.

"Where is my daughter?"

Wong Won secured his daughter at NYU within a couple of minutes. When it came down to his daughter, he wasn't taking any chances so he had her fly back to Hong Kong that night. He of course stayed, hoping that he would be the first person to find Nikolai so that he could have the pleasure of killing her himself.

Ezra also secured his wife, taking her out of the Four Seasons and having her moved to the St. Règis Hotel. Even if he wanted to send Ummah home, she wasn't going for it. She wasn't the kind of wife to leave her husband's side, especially when the war was on. If Ezra had a problem with somebody, then that somebody had two problems instead of one.

Mitch was a little paranoid when he got to his

condo, but once he saw that everything was cool, he moved the cocaine to another secure location. He was pissed off as well, but he knew Nikolai wasn't going anywhere because he had his men demobilize Marco's jet twenty minutes ago. Even if she did leave, Mitch knew what part of Russia she was from and would make it his business to go over there, by himself and put a bullet in her head. Trying to kill his princess was the biggest mistake Nikolai ever made.

"I hate waking him out of his sleep," Davis said, looking at the screen of his phone.

It was late, but Davis needed access to some equipment and the only way he could legally use the devices he was looking to get was if he got permission from his boss, and an OK from a federal judge.

"So do you think a deal is about to go down soon?" Mason asked. "As of yet I haven't seen one transaction, and that fuckin' guy, Ron, vanished off the face of this earth. I don't know how we're gonna get warrants without any probable cause, and Ron's our only evidence."

Mason was right in that respect. Federal judges were careful about what they gave warrants for, mainly because they didn't want anything to fall back on them later on down the line. Without

Ron, it was going to be hard to prove anything illegal was going down. Davis knew something big was going on, and so did Mason, but it wasn't what you knew; it was what they could prove, and right now the only thing Davis and Mason had was a bunch of pictures and a run-away informant who couldn't be found.

"I think we should wait until after the weekend before we call it in. That way it'll give us a little more time to find this fucking guy, Ron," Mason suggested, raising the binoculars up to his eyes and looking out the front windshield.

Davis agreed. It was Friday and the weekend would be over before he knew it. Without Ron he could do nothing anyway, so the surveillance of the Tent had to be put on hold for a minute and now, the new main focus was to find Ron and get him ready to go in front of a judge so that they could get everything that they needed.

Semaj could tell that Qua had an attitude from the minute she pulled into the parking garage of his building. The heavy security she had with her made him even more irritated. The whole situation was getting out of hand and it was taking away from other important things that needed to be dealt with.

"Why you look so mean?" Semaj asked when

she got out of the truck. I thought you would be happy to see me." She smiled.

Semaj found herself about to walk right into Qua's arms, but quickly remembered her security was watching her. A few of them were from Colombia and knew Vikingo well and she didn't want them to see her showing affection to another man. Although she was confused about the way she felt, she did have the right mind not to disrespect her fiancé publicly.

"I'm guessing by now the situation is taken care of," Qua said, looking over Semaj's shoulder at her men standing outside of the trucks.

"Nah, not yet. Dis bitch made a crazy exit right before I was gonna blow her head off," she answered, shaking her head at the thought of how it went down.

"See, that's why you should have let me take care of that when I asked you to. Now you runnin' around... You know what, where is she?" Qua was pretty much fed up with all the bullshit that was going on with Nikolai.

"I don't know. We're working on finding her now," Semaj said. "That's kind of the reason why I'm here."

There were only a few people in this world that made Semaj feel completely safe when she was around them, and Qua was at the top of the list, that is, after Murda Mitch of course. Semaj had no idea how this situation was going to turn out, but the one thing she did know was that she didn't want to go through it by herself.

"You know I love you, right?" Qua mumbled so that only Semaj could hear him.

She smiled and put her head down like a young schoolgirl with a crush. She could never get tired of hearing those words coming from his mouth.

"Are you going to help me?" Semaj asked in an attempt to change the topic.

"Yeah, I'm riding wit' you Maj. Just get rid of your security cause I don't need them around me."

Qua learned that too much security could be very detrimental. First off, it drew a lot of unnecessary attention at times when it wasn't required. Then second, too many guns always prove to be tragic when bullets start flying. That only drew the attention of the police, and the cops were the last people Qua wanted in his business. Ron did enough of that already.

"I think I can take care of that," she said, looking over her shoulders at her men standing by the trucks.

Qua was tempted to reach over and grab Semaj by her waist and pull her close to him. She looked sexy as hell for some reason in her army fatigue. Qua couldn't get enough of her, and already had it embedded in his mind that he was going to get her back one way or another. Right now, he just had to deal with all the bullshit that was going on and once the air was clear he was going all in with Semaj.

Sosa sat in the chair waiting for Blue and Trey to come back from the errand that she sent them on as a diversion. She wanted to be in the house alone when and if Paulette came through. The last thing she wanted to do was scare her off with the armed security walking around the house. Sosa didn't want anything to come in between her and the woman that took her daughter and it was very unfortunate that Patrick was the one that showed up instead.

"You gon' let me bleed to death?" Patrick asked, looking up at Sosa from the floor.

Sosa sat there with a stone look on her face. Patrick had yet to tell her what she wanted to know so his bloody leg and arm really didn't mean anything to her.

"All you gotta do is tell me where my daughter is and I'll take you to a hospital personally," Sosa offered.

"No. Me rather bleed to death. Nyala is the last of an original Jamaican don-dodda. She belong to us."

Sosa looked at him like he was crazy. She could care less about Ox's legacy and last heir to the throne. He was sitting there ranting on about his people and the reason why they needed Nyala so bad. It was all starting to sound like Nyala was a part of some type of ancient myth. Him talking only made Sosa remember how crazy some Jamaicans were as well.

"Nyala is my daughter and I don't care what I gotta do to you, you're gonna tell me where she's at."

Headlights shining through the window caught Sosa's attention. Blue and Trey had finally come back. When they walked into the house, with curiosity on their faces they looked from Sosa to Patrick who was lying on the ground covered in blood.

Blue dropped the bag he had in his hand and immediately pulled his gun from his waist, pointing it at Patrick's chest. Sosa had to damn near jump up from her seat to stop him before he pulled the trigger.

"No! No! Stop!" she yelled out, reaching over and grabbing the bottom of Blue's jacket. "I need to keep him alive. He's the only one who knows where my daughter is," she explained, getting up and standing in between Blue's gun and Patrick.

Sosa thought about the comment Patrick made about rather dying then telling her where Nyala was. If he was dead, her chances of finding Paulette and Nyala were slim to none. She had to preserve his life, even if it was for a temporary time appointed.

"Grab a sheet off one of the beds upstairs," she told Blue, "and bring me down a towel," she shouted, as Blue ran up the steps.

"So now what? You plan on killing me?" Patrick asked, with a creepy grin on his face.

"No, I'm not gonna kill you. I'ma do just the opposite," Sosa answered.

Blue came back downstairs with the sheet and the towel. Sosa directed him to tear the sheet up and wrap his wounds up so that he wouldn't lose any more blood. Seeing what she was trying to do, Patrick tried to put up at struggle. Trey ceased all of that with one swift punch to Patrick's jaw, knocking him straight out. After that, it was easy to patch his wounds up. Blue even bounded Patrick's legs and arms together to stop any further attempts to struggle.

"So, now what?" Blue asked, after tying the final knot at his wrist.

Sosa sat there in a daze for a moment. She was trying to figure out how she was going to get the information out of Patrick. She really didn't know too much about torture because all she ever did was kill, but when she asked Blue and Trey whether or not they ever tortured somebody, Trey stepped up to the plate and was ready with all kinds of tricks up his sleeve.

Chapter 14

"Let me take care of this and then we'll go home and take a nice hot bath," Ezra said, walking up behind Ummah as she stood by the window in their hotel room.

Now that everybody's family was secured, Ezra, Wong Won, and Mitch were on a vicious manhunt for Marco and Nikolai. The funny thing was, neither of them tried to use Marco's jet and according to Mitch's connections at the airport, no flights were leaving out to travel across seas until tomorrow morning. For Ezra, Wong, and Mitch, that means that they were still stuck in the city.

"I hate being this low to the ground," Ummah said, turning around to face him.

"I know, my love. But this is the only room they had on short notice. I promise you that if we're still staying here tomorrow I'll get you another room higher up," Ezra responded, leaning in and kissing her.

"Well you need to be trying to take care of your business so we can go home." Ummah smiled, brushing her thumbs across Ezra's thick eyebrows.

She turned around to take another look at the view and was blinded by a red beam shining through the window. A bullet that came crashing through the glass hit Ummah right under her eye. A second bullet immediately hit her in her chest, knocking her backwards into Ezra's arms. Several more bullets came crashing through the window hitting lamps, mirrors, and even one of Ezra's men who came running over to the window.

"Oh no, baby. Come on, get up," Ezra cried out, cradling Ummah in his arms on the floor.

He wasn't even bothered by the multiple bullets that continued to fly over his head. Another one of Ezra's men ran over and started firing wildly out of the window. It was too dark for him to see anything, but the one thing he could see very clear was the red beam. He got low to the ground real quick, almost being hit by a bullet.

"Ummah, baby. Please baby, don't do this to me!" Ezra continued to cry.

There was blood everywhere and it all came from Ummah. The amount of blood alone was evident enough that she was dead. You couldn't tell Ezra that, though.

"Ezra, we gotta get outta here. She's gone! She's gone!" Ezra's guard yelled out.

Ezra looked down at her body and could see that his guard was right. It only made him mad. He reached over and grabbed the gun from the body of the dead guard.

"Come on, Ezra, she's dead!" the other guard yelled out again, this time grabbing his arm and trying to pull him away from Ummah's body.

Ezra put the gun to the center of his forehead and pulled the trigger, killing him instantly. He then stood up and walked over to the window as though he was on a suicide mission or something. Shock, mixed with a broken heart, had him feeling nothing at all. He stood there looking around for signs of anybody, not caring if he was to be shot. Good thing for him, the shooter had already left moments before he stood up. Ezra just turned around, looked down at Ummah's body one last time then walked out of the room.

"I gotta go check up on Sosa and then we can meet up with my dad," Semaj said to Qua, as they were getting into his car.

Semaj knew the streets of New York better than her security so it wasn't nothing for her to lose them once they took her to pick up her own car. She felt like riding shotgun with Qua was equivalent to any amount of men she had on her security team.

"Maj, can I ask you something," Qua said as

he was driving down the street.

Qua had a lot he wanted to get off his chest pertaining to the way he felt about Semaj. There was no doubt in his mind that he loved her, he was just a little concerned about the way she felt about him. At times he could see that she still had feelings for him and even some love, but it was the amount of love she had, that was in question.

"Do you ever feel like me and you are suppose to be together?" Qua asked, cutting his eyes over at her. "I mean, we've known each other since like, forever and no matter how far life takes up apart, we always find our way back together somehow," Qua went on. "I don't know."

"I think about that all the time, Qua. On some real shit, I never stopped loving you. Through all my trials and tribulations, the love I have for you was the only thing that remained constant. I often think about what my life would be like if me and you were together, and every time I do, I smile."

"Then what's stopping us, Maj?" The conversation was getting a little too deep. So much so, Qua had to pull the car over.

"Qua, I want us to be together and I wish things were different, but the fact still remains that I do got love for Vikingo as well. He's not you, but he's a good man and he treats me right. Hell, I done already cheated on him with you and now I'm suppose to just up and leave him while he's in the hospital because of me. You of all people should know that I'm not that kind of person.

"So you tellin' me that there's no chance for me and you. That's it. You're gonna get married and live happily ever after and say fuck me..."

"No, I'm not sayin' fuck you. I love you. I just... I... I don't know." Semaj sighed.

She was just so confused. Semaj was in love with one man, but felt loyalty towards another. Semaj honestly didn't know what to do. She had never been in a situation like this before, but Qua wasn't going to lay down. He wanted his bitch back and in time he was going to get what he wanted, no matter what the cost was. Semaj knew it too, and loved him so much that she didn't even care.

"Ahhhhhhhhhh, ha, ha, ha. Fuck you. Blood clot muthafucka," Patrick yelled out in pain. "Me don't feel nothin'," he yelled.

Trey had on some latex gloves, digging into Patrick's bullet wounds with his fingers. It hurt, but not enough for Patrick to want to tell Sosa where Nyala and Paulette was. Trey said that he knew how to torture somebody, but none of his tactics were working.

"Alright! Alright. Get him up on the couch," Sosa told Trey and Blue.

She sat on the coffee table right in front of

the couch, looking over at Patrick who was covered in blood and sweat. She should have known this wasn't going to be easy. One thing she gave the Jamaicans credit for, was their toughness. They were capable of enduring a lot of pain and inflicting it as well.

"Where is my daughter?" Sosa asked calmly, as she waved her gun in front of Patrick's face.

Patrick looked over at Sosa and began laughing in her face. Even under extreme circumstances, Patrick was disrespectful, but Sosa wasn't impressed. In fact, it only made her angrier to the point where she wanted to try a few methods of torture that popped up in her head.

Sosa passed her gun to Blue then rolled up her sleeves. It was about to be the amateur hour of torture and Patrick didn't have the slightest idea what he was in for. She was going to just try things that she thought might have hurt.

"Sosa," Trey called out as he came down the steps with her cell phone in his hand. "Somebody's calling."

She grabbed her phone and looked at the screen, not recognizing the number that popped up. For a minute she thought that it was Paulette so she rushed to answer it.

"Yes," she answered with an attitude.

"Hello, Ms. Milano, this is Doctor Craig," the doctor announced, looking down at his chart.

Sosa sat there on the coffee table staring at Patrick while she listened to the doctor explain how Santos checked himself out of the hospital. It shocked the hell out of her considering his injuries, and when she asked, "Who did he leave with?" The doctor was unable to answer that.

"I'ma kill you," Sosa mumbled to herself thinking about how stubborn Santos was.

She sat there and listened to the doctor explain all the risk behind Santos leaving in the condition he was in. He also expressed how important it was for him to come back to the hospital for further treatment. If Sosa knew where he was, she would take him back to the hospital personally. The only problem with that was she didn't have a clue.

"Alright Doc, if he comes home I'll be sure to bring his ass back," Sosa told him before hanging up.

Right when she hung up the phone, headlights flashed through the living room window as a car pulled up into the driveway. Sosa jumped up and dipped behind the partition that separated the living room from the dining room. Blue and Trey both faded away from the window and pulled their guns out, seeing that Patrick even rolled off the couch, not wanting to be hit by any stray bullets that may come crashing through the window.

"Don't nobody shoot unless I say so," Sosa whispered loudly from the dining room.

She didn't know who it was and wasn't about

to take any chances. The headlights went out and the sounds of two car doors slamming could be heard. Everybody sat in silence and waited. Sosa's phone began ringing, getting everyone's attention. Then someone knocked on the door. Sosa nodded for Blue to answer it.

"Yo, who is it?" he yelled, standing off to the side of the door.

"It's Semaj. Is Sosa here?" Semaj said, pulling her Glock from her waist and holding it down by her side.

Qua pulled his weapon, too, and so did Murda Mitch. Everybody was on high alert, and when Blue opened the door, a sigh of relief came over everybody.

"Damn nigga, I didn't recognize your voice," Mitch said, throwing a playful jab at Blue.

"Damn, Sosa! What da hell is goin' on in here and who da fuck is this?" Semaj asked, pointing her gun down at Patrick lying on the floor.

Mitch and Qua walked over and stood above Patrick, looking down at him like he was an alien of some sort. From the dreads, Qua already knew it had something to do with Ox—that and the fact Semaj gave him a brief update about Nyala's kidnapping.

"He knows where Nyala is. I think he's the one that took her," Sosa said, walking over and giving Patrick a swift kick to the gut. "He's not sayin' shit though. Aye, by the way, do either of y'all two know anything about torture?" Sosa asked Mitch and Qua.

Desperate times called for desperate measures and at this point Sosa would do anything to get Patrick to talk. The more time they wasted messing around with him, the further away Paulette was taking Nyala. Something had to give and it had to give now, and just by chance, Sosa was in luck.

"I think I might be able to make him talk," Murda Mitch said, taking off his jacket and passing it to Semaj.

"Yeah, I picked up a few things while I was in London myself," Qua added, also removing his jacket.

It was easy for Nikolai and Marco to become like ghosts in the city. They stayed at a house Marco purchased a couple of years back in Albany, New York. He bought the house because his gunrunning business picked up on the East Coast and often, he would stay in the States for weeks at a time conducting business. If he wanted to avoid hotels for any reason, that's where he would stay and it was low-key and out of the way, just the way he liked it.

"You might wanna get some sleep. We got a long day ahead of us," Marco told Nikolai when he walked into the guest room where she was.

She hadn't had any sleep for over 26 hours and her body still didn't show any signs of fatigue. Marco looked on as she broke down and cleaned several guns lying on the bed. A lit cigarette dangled from her mouth and a light perspiration began to build up around her neck. It was kind of a turn on to see Nikolai in this fashion.

"Is it worth it?" Marco inquired as he was on his way back out of the room.

"What?" Nikolai responded, cocking a bullet into the chamber of one of the assault rifles.

Marco stopped at the door and turned around to face her. "All of this," he said, waving at all the guns. "Was what you did worth you having to go through all of this?"

Nikolai heard the question and it made her think. She tossed the rifle down onto the bed then put both of her hands into her back pockets. Looking down at the guns then back up at Marco, she answered, "You of all people should know what I'm after right now." Slowly, she walked over towards him.

"Yeah and what's that?"

"Power," she replied, nodding her head. "Men crave it every second of the day, but only few possess it."

Nikolai's plot was deeper than what everybody thought. Not only did she want to take over Colombia, she wanted to wipe out and rebuild the whole 16 Tent with her being the head of it. In doing so, she would have more power than one female could handle, not to mention she would become a billionaire practically overnight. With that kind of money and power not only would Nikolai have control over Colombia and parts of the United States, she would also be in a position to bring Russia, her homeland, to its knees. The sky was the limit and the only thing she needed to do was finish what she'd started.

Chapter 15

Paulette didn't want to move Nyala since her face was still planted on the television screen, but she had to keep it moving if she wanted to catch the boat that was leaving out in less than 24 hours.

"Nyala, baby. Come on, we gotta go," Paulette yelled out to the bathroom where Nyala was brushing her teeth.

Paulette stuffed clothes and their other belongings into bags. It was just after 7am and Paulette thought that it would be smart to get on the road now in order to get a jump on the hectic Saturday traffic.

"Auntie P, can we call my auntie Maj," Nyala asked when she came out of the bathroom.

"Who you say?" Paulette asked, not really hearing the name that she said.

"My auntie Maj. Can I stay with her?" Nyala asked, taking a seat on the bed.

Paulette didn't know who Semaj was and

really didn't care for that matter. It kind of made her a little mad that Nyala would ask to stay with someone else other than her, but she kept her cool and didn't show how angry she was about the comment.

"How about you stay with Auntie P for a little while and then we'll find ya auntie Maj in a couple of weeks—"

"I know her number. We can just call her," Nyala pleaded, cutting Paulette off.

Nyala really wasn't trying to hear what Paulette was talking about. She knew her, but not that well. She was closer to Semaj and if she had to stay with anybody, she would want to stay with her. Paulette saw how she felt and hated it.

"What's her number? Let's give ya auntie Maj a call," Paulette said, pulling out her phone.

Nyala ran the number down to her while Paulette faked like she was calling her. She put the phone to her ear then got up from the bed as though she was talking. Nyala watched and listened to Paulette from the bed.

"Yeah, Maj, I got her... I know it's crazy what happened to Sosa... We'll be back for the funeral... No, she's right here. You wanna talk to her? I know, Maj, stop cryin'... Well, she said she wanted to come stay wit you... You're about to go out of town? I know, I know... Well, she don't need anything... Okay, I'll let her know what you said... Okay then,

I'll give you a call later," Paulette said then faked like she was hanging up the phone.

She walked back over to the bed and sat down next to Nyala, putting her arm around her. "Ya auntie Maj said that she was going to be busy for the next couple of weeks, but she said she will come get you then. She wanted me to tell you that she loves you very much and the reason why she didn't want to talk to you was because she didn't want to make you cry because she was crying," Paulette lied, kissing Nyala on her forehead.

Paulette thought that she was slick. She thought that it would be easy pulling the wool over the young child's eyes, but she was wrong. Nyala wasn't just your typical kid. She was smart as hell, and she knew beyond a shadow of a doubt that Paulette hadn't talked to Semaj. Nyala knew it because she purposely gave Paulette the wrong number. In fact, she gave Paulette Santos's house number. She really just wanted to see if her mom would pick up the phone. When Paulette went into her fake conversation with Semaj, Nyala knew that Paulette was a liar and that something was wrong. She didn't want to let Paulette know that she knew, but if the opportunity ever presented itself, Nyala was going to run for it, or at least call the police for help. Until that time came, she wasn't going to say anything. She was going to continue to play Paulette's game to the fullest without any signs of suspicion.

Patrick woke up to the excruciating pain of his eighth fingernail being pulled off by Murda Mitch with a pair of pliers. This one hurt so badly that Patrick pissed on himself. Qua was there to douse his finger with rubbing alcohol to make it hurt even more. Patrick tried to pass out like he did after the fourth fingernail, but Mitch wouldn't let him this time. He put the small stick of smelling salts under his nose, which woke him right up. A couple smacks to the face topped it off.

"Rude boy, you got two more fingers and ten more toes. After that, I'ma nurse you back to good health then try something else on you," Mitch said, kneeling down beside him. "Just tell me where she's at and I'll stop. We'll even drop you off at the hospital," Mitch bargained.

Between the beating he took from Trey, the two bullet wounds and now eight of his fingernails being pulled off, Patrick was starting to consider talking. He wasn't quite at that point yet, but as soon as Mitch reached down and grabbed his finger, Patrick bitched up.

"Wait!" he yelled, squirming from the pain. "I think she might be in Florida."

"Nah. That's not what I'm looking for," Mitch said, putting the pliers up to his fingers.

Mitch didn't want half or partial information.

He wanted it all with specific directions how to get there. Anything else wasn't worth listening to.

"Okay! Okay!" Patrick yelled. "She's in Atlanta right now, at a motel called Riverside Inn—two miles south of the airport," Patrick explained. "I'm suppose to meet up with her in Florida, right off I-95 at the Fair Hill Motel," Patrick confessed.

Mitch let his hand go and pulled the pliers back. "You better not be lying," Mitch said, taking a seat in the chair. "Sosa!" Mitch yelled into the living room where everybody else was.

Sosa had nodded off for a minute, but woke up when she heard her name being called. She jumped up and headed to where everyone was.

Once they surrounded Patrick, he began to tell them everything, starting with how all of this was Paulette's idea. He didn't leave out any details about the whole plan of getting Nyala back to Jamaica where Paulette felt that she belonged.

"The jet is already gassed up. We can be in Atlanta in less than two hours," Semaj said, jumping to her phone to make the flight arrangements.

Sosa immediately pulled out her gun, placing it to the center of Patrick's head. She was about to pull the trigger, but Mitch stuck his hand out to stop her. It wasn't that Mitch didn't want her to kill him, because he could care less about Patrick, he just wanted to make sure that they got Nyala back first. He really didn't have to explain that to Sosa because once she thought about it, she lowered her weapon.

"You better not be lying," she threatened before walking out of the kitchen.

Ron walked out onto the roof of an apartment building and took in a deep breath. He made his way over to the ledge, looking out at all the cars driving by and the few pedestrians walking up and down the street. Ron had a lot on his mind and was stressed to the max. For a moment, he actually wanted to throw himself off the roof, feeling that doing so would be less painful than being labeled as a snitch.

"Damn!" Ron yelled out, swinging into the air.

He scratched his head and paced back and forth on the roof, honestly not knowing what he was going to do. Even though he wasn't giving them any more information, Ron knew that the feds were still watching Qua. The last person he wanted to get booked was him. Before all of this happened, they were like family. His mother really looked at and treated Qua like he was her son. For Ron to possibly be the reason why Qua would see the inside of the federal jail was crushing him.

"Come on, Ron, think," he barked, rocking back and forth on the ledge.

He had to make something happen ASAP

and he knew it. Other than that, it would only be a matter of time until they came for Qua and whoever else he was dealing with. Ron needed to speak to Agent Davis. He had another plan in mind and knew that this one would keep Qua out of jail, just as long as Davis played ball by his rules. Ron was at the end of his rope and if this didn't work, then jumping off this building would be his last and final option.

Semaj looked over at Sosa, who was looking out of the jet window at the clouds floating in the sky well below the aircraft. She could see the stress in Sosa's eyes and could only imagine the pain that she was going through having her only child taken away from her.

"We're going to get her back," Semaj assured Sosa, reaching over and placing her hand over the top of hers.

Sosa looked like she wanted to break down, but she held it together feeling that crying right now wasn't going to make the situation any better. Semaj admired that about Sosa. Even when faced with adversity, Sosa always kept her cool.

"I just want her back, you know," Sosa said, fighting back tears. "Let me ask you something, Maj. When you lost Niran, how did you cope with it?"

Semaj put her head down. It had been a long

time since she thought about the day her baby boy was murdered in a vicious car bomb that took his, and her uncle Paulie's life.

"It was hard at first, but then I realized that the only way I was going to be able to move on with my life was if I gained some type of control over my grief. He was my world, but at the same time I had other responsibilities. The Milano family needed me and if I would have focused on Niran's death, I probably would have been buried right next to him by now," Semaj told her, wiping the single tear that fell down her cheek.

Sosa was amazed at how strong she was. Semaj didn't know it, but Sosa was the one who looked up to and admired her strength and courage all these years. She watched Semaj go from being a wild young girl, to becoming a woman not to be fucked with—a boss nonetheless.

"So what's going on with Nikolai?" Sosa asked, trying to change the subject before her feelings and emotions started to get the best of her.

"I'm not gonna lie. That bitch crazy." Semaj chuckled, shaking her head. "I should have put a bullet in her head a long time ago," she said, throwing back the shot of Hennessey she was holding on to.

"Yeah, Marco's ass, too," Sosa added.

"But it's cool. As soon as we get Nyala back, I'ma take care of that. She thinks I don't know where she's at and I want it to stay that way." Semaj smiled.

Turns out the house that Marco bought in Albany—Semaj was the one that recommended it to him when it first went on the market. Nyala was the only reason why Semaj didn't have a hundred men running down on the house. Family always came first, and besides, the beef she had with Nikolai and Marco was personal. For now, killing them could wait, but it was going to get done if it was the last thing Semaj did.

Ezra looked down into the wooden box Ummah's body was lying in. Today, he was sending her back to Africa so that she could be buried in their homeland. With his private jet ready to take off and his family at home waiting for her return, Ezra leaned in and kissed her stiff, cold lips for the last time. He was sure that he wasn't going to see her again in this life and probably in the hereafter because what he was about to do was guaranteed to have him burn in hell. Not only did he plan on killing Nikolai and Marco, he was going to extend his favor to both their families. Ezra was hot and the only thing on his mind right now was revenge.

"Ezra, we might have a hit on her cell phone," one of Ezra's people informed him. "I have a team of men who are ready to move on it now," he said, looking down into the box at a woman and many other young, poor Africans.

"No, I'm going alone," Ezra told him. "Just get me the address to where he's at and I'll take care of the rest," Ezra responded without taking his eyes off the box.

Africans were up on the technology with cell phones and found a way to track Marco's cell phone down by using the GPS already manufactured into his phone. They got the phone's location narrowed down to a one-block radius. The house or building could not be specified, but it didn't matter if Ezra had to kick in every door on that street, he was going to do it.

"I trust you, Kaylo. I want you to go back to Africa with my wife and make sure she gets a proper burial," he said, sticking his hand out for a shake.

Kaylo didn't want to leave Ezra behind for fear that he, too, was going to end up in a wooden box. The thing was, Ezra didn't care if he lived or died at this point, just as long as he could watch the life drift out of Nikolai's body as he choked her to death. All Ezra saw was red, and red only meant murder.

"You're not gonna believe who just called me," Davis said, walking up to Mason's desk. "Ron, and he said he got something big for us."

He was a little excited because up until now,

they hadn't heard anything from Ron and weren't sure if he was dead or alive. Not only was he alive, he let Davis know that he'd been working on something that was huge. Davis was hoping that Ron had information on Sosa, or possibly even Qua, since he was officially on the FBI watch list as well. Whatever it was, Davis needed it because his case was starting to go cold. Anything at this point would be helpful. Ron knew it too, and was banking on Davis's greed to open a door for him to rid his name of being dirt on these streets.

Chapter 16

"Yo dog, you don't look too good. I'm about to get you to the hospital," CJ looked over and told Santos, who was fading in and out of consciousness in the passenger seat.

Santos had bags under his eyes and his skin was pale to the point where it looked like he dipped his face in a bag of flower. He appeared to be about five minutes away from dying, but even so, he still wanted to keep pushing. Santos was starting to remind CJ of Denzel Washington when he played in the movie *Man on Fire*, except Denzel was only acting.

"Man, just keep driving. We're almost there," Santos said, unscrewing the bottle of pills he had in his hand. "Make sure you get off on the right exit."

Everything Patrick said played back in Santos's head over and over again. He was going to save Nyala at all cost or he was going to at least die trying. The excruciating pain from the bullet wound to his chest had him popping pills like they were candy. He refused to give up now, though. He came too far and endured too much to turn around. He was on one.

"That's the exit right there," Santos said, nodding at the large green sign posted on the side of the highway.

CJ got off the exit as directed. The exit took them to a road that was lined with strip malls. There were all kinds of hotels and motels just about everywhere and CJ even drove past a hospital, which he desperately wanted to take Santos into to get checked out.

"Yo, what was the name of the motel again?" CJ asked, looking out his window at several of them lined up back to back.

"The Fair Hill Inn, do you see one?" Santos asked, looking out the window at all the motels. "He said it was right by the exit so it gotta be here."

About a mile down the road and to his right, CJ finally saw the motel. Funny thing was that as soon as CJ pulled into the parking lot, Santos noticed another Fair Hill Motel not too far down the road. Now he was confused because he didn't know which one Nyala was stashed at. As CJ pulled into the parking lot, Santos threw his head back and began thinking about what he should do next.

Wong Won drove through lower Manhattan three cars deep, on his way into Chinatown. His people there said that an older woman with an accent came by one of his establishments looking for him. She said to tell Wong to contact her immediately because it was important. Wong knew who it was, but he didn't have much to say. He was only hoping Nikolai was still in the area.

"Park on Canal Street, we'll get out and walk from there," Wong yelled from the back seat.

Nikolai knew that Wong Won ran Chinatown, but it was only one particular spot Wong ever invited her to and that was a Chinese sweatshop he had operating in the basement of one of his restaurants.

"Alright, spread out," Wong said as he and the rest of his men got out of their cars. "I got two million for anybody that kills her, and one million for anybody who kills Marco," Wong offered up, as he ever so smoothly put his dark sunglasses over his eyes.

One thing about Wong, he didn't care how the job got done. Yes, it was personal, but not to the point where he needed to be the one who actually pulled the trigger.

Out of all three cars, Wong had about eight men with him total. As they walked down Canal Street, six of his men branched off while the other two men stayed with Wong. The six men began checking stores immediately, hoping they would catch Nikolai or Marco slipping. Anybody with a million dollars on their head was liable to get a face shot from either of his men who not only wanted the money, but also wanted to please Wong with their work.

"Let's go around back," Wong said, looking up at his restaurant.

The back was the way to the sweatshop and once they saw who it was standing at the door, it was opened. The sounds of sewing machines filled the air as women and men worked their fingers to the bone. Everybody's head was down, focusing on their work, so Wong really couldn't see what was lurking in the shadows for him.

The manager came out of his office to meet Wong with a bow. Off the bat he was jittery and nervous and it didn't take much for Wong to notice that. "So what happened earlier with the women that came by?" Wong asked, looking around the shop at the workers.

The manager was scared to death so he started speaking in his native tongue hoping he could disguise what he was going to tell Wong. Unfortunately, he didn't know that Nikolai spoke four other languages other than Russian, and Chinese was one of them.

The extra large straw hat she had on allowed her to go unnoticed, but as soon as the manager began warning Wong of her presence, Nikolai raised up from one of the sewing machines with two 17 shot Glock 9mms and began letting it fly in Wong's direction.

Pop! Pop! Pop! Pop! Pop! Pop! Pop! Pop! Pop! Pop!

Two of Nikolai's men who were also disguised as workers, hopped up and began firing in Wong's direction as well. Needless to say, Wong and his men scattered like roaches, pulling their weapons and diving behind tables and partitions. Other shop workers also dropped to the floor to avoid being hit by the many bullets being fired.

"Nikolai, I'ma fuckin' kill you," Wong belted over the loud roar of his opponents gun blasts.

One of Wong's men jumped up from behind the table to try and return fire, but was tagged by Nikolai before he could get a shot off. Nikolai was like a surgeon with the two bulky handguns equipped with infrared beams. Seeing the red lasers streaming across the room, Wong wasn't stupid enough to just pop up from behind the partition he hid behind.

A small piece of relief came when the manager stormed out of his office with a pump action gauge. Nikolai didn't even have time to turn around and shoot him so she did the only thing she could do which was try to get out the way.

MAFIA *Princess* PART 5

Boom! Cha-cha Boom! Cha-cha Boom!

Blue flames spit out the shotgun as it blasted holes in tables, tore apart a sewing machine, and damn near hit Nikolai before she dove to the floor. The manager was tagged by one of Nikolai's men before he could do any more damage, and while Nikolai's man shot the manager, he too was hit by Wong who saw the opportunity and popped up from behind the partition.

Bullets were flying in every direction and for a moment it looked as though Wong and his men had gotten the upper hand. Then it happened. Nikolai's man fired a single shot, blindly from under the table he was ducking behind, and hit Wong in his stomach. The bullet entered him and Wong felt like his stomach was on fire the way the hot lead ball moved around inside of him. He dropped down to one knee.

One of Wong's men tried to attend to him, but was hit by Nikolai as he ran over to Wong. The second of Wong's men was so mad he jumped up and began walking across the tables, firing down on Nikolai's men.

"Ahhhhhhh!" the man yelled, as he continued firing. "Fuck you, mudafucka. Fuck you!" he shouted.

Nikolai muffled his bark, firing two shots and hitting him on the side of his head as he ran right past her. His body dropped to the ground. One of Nikolai's men jumped up from the floor, aiming his gun across the room. Nikolai and he spotted Wong sitting on the floor with his back up against the wall.

Nikolai was a little smarter than her man. Seeing that Wong still had his gun in his hand, she wasn't so quick to run up on him. He played possum and Nikolai's man went for it. As soon as he got close enough, Wong raised the gun and began firing what bullets he had left in his gun. His body dropped right beside Wong's and as fast as he could, Wong tried to reload his gun.

"No, no, no," Nikolai said, slowly walking up on Wong, reaching him before he could get the fresh clip into the gun.

Wong looked up into her eyes and could see that it was too late. He didn't even attempt to try and load his weapon. In fact, he placed the gun and the clip on the ground beside him. There was no need to try and play Superman when the end result was him being killed by her inevitably. At this point, all he wanted to do was try and get some answers before he checked out.

"Why?" Wong asked, placing his hand over the bullet wound to his stomach. "Why would you…" Wong was unable to complete the sentence as he became too weak.

Nikolai wasn't trying to answer any questions, nor did she wanna hear Wong talk for that matter. She raised the gun up and pointed it to the center of his forehead. The red dot was right in between his eyebrows. Not another moment was wasted as Nikolai squeezed the trigger at point blank range.

"Alright, me and Qua gone get a rental car and check the motels in the area. I'll call the airport in Florida and reserve you a rental. Take Trey wit' you and make sure you call me as soon as the plane land," Semaj instructed Sosa before her and Qua got off the jet. "Be careful," Semaj shouted before the door went up.

It was agreed upon by everybody that the best thing to do at this point was to split up. Nyala could have been in either Atlanta or Florida right now and it wouldn't have made much sense for everyone to be looking for her in the same place.

"Call me," Semaj mouthed to Sosa through the window as the jet began to pull back out.

Qua and Semaj had a little distance to walk in order to get out the rental car place, which was located on the other side of the airport. Qua trailed behind Semaj, only because he had a quick phone call to make and didn't want her to hear his conversation.

"Yo, my nigga. Is you still checking up on that situation I told you to keep yo' eyes on?"

"I got you. I'm still on point," the man reassured Qua.

"Alright. Well I need you to make sure that's taken care of for me," Qua told him before hanging up the phone.

Nothing else needed to be said. Qua had put a set of wheels in motion and there wasn't no stopping them. As much as he loved Semaj, he didn't want to anyway. In order for them to be together a sacrifice had to be made and Qua was willing to make that sacrifice even if that meant that he could possibly lose Semaj forever.

"Who was that?" Semaj asked, turning around to see Qua jogging up behind her.

"I was just checking up on Ron. You know, I'm gonna have to deal with that shit once I get back home."

Semaj looked in Qua's eyes and before she could ask him anything else he turned away. She definitely thought he was up to something, but she had so many other things on her mind she didn't have the energy to try and figure it out. But Semaj trusted Qua with her life, so whatever it was, she knew he had her best interest at heart.

"You think Paulette gonna just give Nyala back without a fight," Patrick stated to Murda Mitch, who was sitting on the couch flipping through the TV stations.

Mitch got stuck with the babysitting duties since he didn't feel like doing that nonstop flying and driving all day. It didn't have anything to do with Nyala because in his heart he really wanted her back home with Sosa. Mitch just didn't feel like his body was up for all the physical pressure and he felt like his age was starting to catch up with him.

"Her gonna kill Sosa when she see her. Paulette love dat little girl more than anything in the world," Patrick warned.

"How about you just shut da fuck up and let me find something on TV," Mitch shot back, not interested at all in listening to Patrick ramble on.

Mitch knew beyond a shadow of a doubt that if Sosa caught up with Paulette, she was as good as dead. The love that she had in her heart for her daughter far outweighed any love Paulette thought she had for Nyala. As her mother, Sosa was willing to go the distance, and would kill anything and anybody that stood in the way of her bringing her baby home.

"Who da hell is..." Mitch said, feeling his phone vibrate in his jacket pocket. He didn't notice the number that popped up on the screen. "Who this," he answered, as he continued to change the channels.

"Mitch, it's me Marco."

Mitch stopped playing with the television and got serious after hearing Marco's voice. "What you callin' my phone for?"

"I need to ask you something and I need you to keep it... Let me see how I can say this... I want you to keep it 100 with me," Marco said, digging deep into his street language vocabulary.

"Yeah, wassup Marco," Mitch said, getting up from the couch and looking around the house suspiciously.

"Do y'all really plan on killing me too?" Marco asked.

Mitch hesitated answering the question, walking over to the window and peaking out the blinds. There wasn't anybody outside and Mitch didn't think Marco would try to do anything in broad daylight. So with that, Mitch kept it 100.

"You might wanna call home and tell ya family to pick out a plot for you. You tried to kill my little girl and I swear just as water is wet, I'ma blow ya fuckin' head off," Mitch said, then hung up the phone.

Five seconds didn't even go by before a bullet came crashing through the front window, grazing Mitch's right shoulder. Two seconds later, the back door was being kicked in and a few more bullets pierced the window. Mitch got low to the ground and pulled his weapon. Two masked men stormed into the house from the back door with MP-5s in their hands.

Mitch darted up the steps, firing a couple of shots at the men to try and slow them down. It had the total opposite effect because they let it rip.

"Yeah, mon! Kill da blood clot, mudafucka!" Patrick yelled out from the floor.

The gunmen were coming to kill everything in the house that was breathing, so Patrick was included no matter what the circumstances were. He was shot over ten times as they walked over his body on their way up the steps. He died instantly.

Once the men got up the steps they both looked up and down the empty hallway. One of the men headed towards the back room while the other eased his way towards the front room. They knew that they didn't have much time left before the cops would be called by the neighbors so they had to move fast, kill Mitch, and get out of there.

The one gunman who was headed towards the front room passed by the hallway bathroom, pushing the door open and sticking the gun inside. Mitch was in the closet right across from the bathroom. He eased the door open, pointed the gun to the back of the gunman's head, and pulled the trigger. Pop! Pop! Pop!

All three bullets hit him in his head causing his body to fall face first onto the bathroom floor. The second gunman spun around and the only thing he could see was his partner's legs halfway out the bathroom door. He let fear get the best of him, knowing that his partner was dead, so he started firing wildly into the direction of the front room as he made a break for the steps.

Mitch stayed in the closet until he heard the front door open then shut. His cell phone went off in his pocket again and out of curiosity Mitch reached into his pocket and answered it.

"You still alive I assume," Marco said into the phone, watching the second gunman running towards him.

"Is that all you got?" Mitch replied, easing his way out of the closet. "You might wanna come back and collect your dead friend," he taunted, kicking the gunman's lifeless body.

"See that's the thing you don't get, Mitch. I have hundreds of men willing to do this as often as I need them to," he said, getting his weapon and pointing it at the second gunmen's head before pulling the trigger.

The bullet entered the front of his skull then exited out the top of it, collapsing his body right by Marco's feet. He did that for two reasons. One, because he ran out of the house like a little bitch, and two, he left a good man behind. Mitch heard the shot and shook his head.

"If you think for a split second I'ma just let y'all kill me, you got another thing coming. You might wanna buy a couple of suits cause there's going to be a lot of funerals," Marco said, then hung up the phone.

Mitch wasn't sweet by a long shot, but at the same time he knew when he had a problem on his hand. Marco didn't have more money than Mitch and his daughter, but what he did have was more valuable than money. Marco had guns and plenty of them on deck, and not just that, he had an unlimited amount of men that were still ready to kill or die for him. That's what made Marco a problem and Mitch respected it.

Chapter 17

Cigarette smoke filled Ron's Range Rover as he lit up Newports back to back. He was nervous and didn't have the slightest idea how the day was going to end. Nothing good ever came from dealing with the feds and Ron felt it was only by luck that nobody in the streets had taken matters into their own hands and put a bullet in his head by now. That was common for the young thugs in this day and time, especially the gang members who lived by the strict code of not being a rat.

Ron looked into his rearview mirror then over at his phone sitting in the center console. Agent Davis hadn't showed up yet, so while he was sitting there he decided to call Qua. They hadn't spoken since the night Qua found out he was an informant. He became even more nervous once Qua's phone started to ring.

"Yo, who dis?" Qua answered looking at the blocked number showing up on his screen.

"Qua, don't hang up on me," Ron pleaded from

the rip.

"Fuck you want, nigga? I told you not to call my phone," Qua popped.

"I know bro, but I gotta holla at you. It's important."

Semaj reached over and tapped Qua, letting him know that they were at the motel. She pulled into the parking lot and reached under her seat to retrieve a black and grey, compact .45 automatic. Qua looked up at the motel with the phone still in his hand.

"You got one minute, nigga," he told Ron, as he too reached under his seat and grabbed his all chrome .40 caliber Smith & Wesson.

Ron began venting. "Bro, I know I fucked up big time. It's no excuse for the shit I did and I know you might not ever forgive me, but at least let me get a chance to make dis shit right."

"And what can you possibly do to make me forget that you are a rat?" Qua harshly replied.

Ron clenched his teeth in frustration. He hated being labeled as a snitch or a rat. It was the worst thing you could be in the hood and Ron was feeling the consequences of his choices in the worst way.

"Look, I can't tell you what's goin' on right now, but just know that after today, you and yo' folks should be straight." Ron stopped talking for a second when he noticed headlights turning down the block. "Look man, I gotta go. No matter what happens, I love you, brah and that's real," Ron said, then hung up the phone.

He took another pull of the cigarette before getting out of the car. Davis had parked a couple of cars back, but flashed his lights a few times to let Ron know that it was him.

"Got damn Ron, where the hell you been?" Mason asked, slamming the passenger side door.

"Yeah you been M.I.A. lately," Davis chimed in, walking over to Ron like he was about to try and search him.

Ron wasn't going for it though. He backed up and smacked Davis's hand down. Davis looked at him like he was crazy, but Ron wasn't crazy, he was confident about what he had to offer.

"Look, I ain't come here for all that," Ron said walking over and leaning up against Davis's car.

"Well, what you got then, and it better be good," Davis spoke, walking up and standing right in front of him.

"Yeah, well, before we even get into all of that, let me tell you what I want from you," Ron said. "That little bit of evidence you got on me needs to magically disappear. As a matter of fact, I want it back in my possession so I can get rid of it myself."

"You musta bumped ya head." Mason laughed, digging in his jacket pocket to grab a cigarette.

"Yeah and I woke up remembering where 500 kilos of raw, uncut, Colombian cocaine is at," Ron told them.

If he didn't before, now Ron really got Davis's attention. Those kinds of numbers could only mean that a cartel was involved. This sounded like the break that he needed.

"I'm listening," Davis said, giving Ron his full, undivided attention.

"You know that guy, Qua, I was rolling with. He's really the man in New York. He's right under Sosa and I can bring down his whole operation like that," Ron said with a snap of a finger. "I'm talking over 30 major drug dealers that control parts of every borough, all under the leadership of Qua, and I know where three of his stash houses are, one of which is holding 500 kilos," Ron explained.

Davis didn't want to show it, but he was excited about the new information. "All you want in return is the evidence I took from you?" Davis questioned, needing confirmation.

"Yeah, that's it and I want y'all to leave me da fuck alone."

Davis didn't even have to think twice about it. The cost of bringing down a multi-million dollar drug operation was cheap in comparison to what Ron was asking for. Davis still had that stuff in his trunk and was tempted to give it up on the spot, but decided against it. Ron had to put up first before Davis gave him anything.

When Semaj showed the clerk at the front desk a picture of Nyala, he knew exactly who she was. It had only been a few hours since Paulette checked in. He remembered seeing the little girl wiping some tears from her face while she stood next to Paulette as she was paying the bill. He even remembered the clothes Nyala had on.

"Sosa didn't land yet, and she probably doesn't have her phone on," Semaj said, walking back outside where Qua was leaning up against the rental car.

"You think she's on her way to Florida?"

"She gotta be," the dude back at the house said that he was suppose to meet her in Florida... Hold on," Semaj said, reaching in her back pocket to get her vibrating phone. "Hi, Daddy!" she answered, seeing that it was Mitch.

"It's official. We're definitely at war with Marco and Nikolai," Mitch said, standing across the street from Wong Won's restaurant. "They just tried to kill me."

He watched as the coroner brought body after body out from the basement along with some of the Chinese workers who were illegal immigrants. There had to be about 15 cop cars lined up and down the street, and of course, nobody knew anything.

"Did y'all find Nyala yet?" Mitch asked.

"No, not yet. They weren't in Atlanta. We think they might already be on their way to Florida,"

Semaj answered.

"Yeah well, Marco's men killed the Jamaican at the house so y'all gotta work with what y'all got. Oh and Wong Won is dead too," Mitch added, looking at all the Chinese men in suits standing in front of the building with solemn looks across their faces.

"If you need me to, I can come..."

"Nah, nah. I'm good. I'm going to take care of the problem myself. Y'all just find that little girl and bring her back," Mitch said, hanging up the phone before Semaj could say anything.

He knew that she would have tried to convince him to chill out until they got back, but Mitch was dead on that. The attempt on his life had made Mitch want to go right back to being the lethal killer he used to be. Once the beef was on, there was no turning back for Mitch until he tasted blood.

Vikingo lay in his hospital bed, periodically looking up at the television in the corner of the room, but his mind was somewhere else. He wondered what Semaj was doing. She hadn't been back to visit him in a couple of days, now she wasn't answering his calls. He was going through it.

"Vikingo, I'ma get something to eat. Do you want something?" Tito asked, coming into the room.

Vikingo shook his head and waved Tito off. He wasn't hungry the least bit nor did he feel like having anybody around him right now. He already dismissed Raphael—the other guard that was supposed to be watching over him. Right now, Vikingo preferred not to have anyone in his space. He definitely didn't want his men to see him cry because that's exactly what he felt like doing.

"Nurse!" Vikingo yelled out, pushing the little button.

When she came in, he directed her to turn the TV off, close the blinds and shut his door. He wanted to be alone, in the dark, and he didn't want to be disturbed by anyone. He was stressed out thinking that he had lost the woman that he loved. Thoughts of the wedding and starting a family with Semaj filled his head. The tears automatically began falling down his face. He sat up and punched down on his legs in a rage of anger and wasn't able to feel anything.

The door handle turning caught his attention. He hurried up and wiped the tears from his face, hoping whomever it was coming through the door didn't see him like this. "Hold up, I don't want any company right now," Vikingo said, waving his hand at the man coming into the room.

The man ignored him. Without saying a word he reached into his jacket and pulled a black 9mm with a silencer on it. Vikingo knew that this was it for him. He pushed the nurse's button, but it didn't matter, he was too late. The man raised the gun up and squeezed the trigger.

Pew! Pew! Pew! Pew! Vikingo got hit with all four shots in his chest. When he inhaled, Vikingo could taste the gunpowder in his throat. He looked up and could see the man walking up to the side of his bed. He saw the gun even clearer when it was pointed directly at his face.

Vikingo tried to say something, but his lungs were starting to fill up with blood. The gunman pressed the silencer up against his forehead and pulled the trigger. Brain fragments and blood splattered all over his pillows, and just as swift as the gunman walked into the room, he walked out in the same manner.

"You think this guy's pulling our chain," Mason asked, looking through a pair of binoculars at a house at the corner of the block.

In good faith, Ron gave them the address to one of Qua's stash houses in the Bronx. It was the smallest stash house Qua had but it held a lot of weight. He wasn't going to give up anything else unless he got what he wanted. Ron only gave up this location as a teaser to pull the detectives in.

"We sure as hell gon' find out," Davis said, looking down at his watch.

Ron informed them that a large delivery was going to be made to the house at a certain time, along with the pick-up of a larger amount of money. The heavy security Ron warned them of was also present.

"Hold up, I think we got action," Mason said, putting the binoculars back up to his eyes.

A cherry red F-150 pulled up to the stash house. The men, who were standing in front, pulled their weapons and spread out around the truck. Davis quickly realized that the men were there for security purposes and were waiting for this truck to pull up.

"Here we go," Davis said, as he looked through his set of binoculars. "That's it," he mumbled.

The driver never got out of the truck, only the passenger who pulled two, large, black duffle bags out of the cabin and tossed them onto the pavement. Moments later another man emerged from the house with his own duffle bag over his shoulder. The exchange of bags was fast with little conversation and before Davis knew it, the passenger jumped back into the truck and the driver pulled off. Everything Ron told them was the truth and his timing was on point.

"So what now?" Mason asked, watching the truck roll down the street, but not before getting the license plate number.

Davis looked over at him and smiled. "I think it's time we give Ron what he wants," Davis said, then threw the car in drive and slowly pulled out of his parking space.

Chapter 18

"Dog, you sure this the right motel?" CJ asked, getting back into the car. "The manager looked at the picture and said that she didn't see Nyala."

"This gotta be it. I know what I heard," Santos said in a low tone before popping another painkiller.

Santos was running out of pain medicine and his injuries were starting to get worse. If he didn't get to a hospital in the very near future, his chances of surviving were going to be slim to none.

"Yo, you should let me get you to a hospital," CJ said, looking over at him. "You look like you about to die," he said in all seriousness.

Santos smiled then turned to look out of the window. He thought that his eyes were deceiving him when he saw a Chrysler 300 with New York tags pull into a parking spot across the way from where he was. He blinked real hard to readjust his eyes to make sure he saw what he thought he did.

It was, clear as day, a New York state license plate.

"Look, son," Santos said, pointing at the car.

As soon as he said that, Paulette and Nyala got out of the car with Burger King bags in their hands. Santos almost had a heart attack seeing Nyala.

"Yo, dat's her, son," CJ said, attempting to exit the car to go and grab her.

Santos stopped him before he could. He noticed when Paulette got out of the car she stuffed a gun into her waist. He didn't want to take the chance of getting into a shootout with Nyala so close by. Instead, he just let her and Nyala go into the motel room.

"We gotta do something," CJ said, pulling out his gun and sitting it on his lap.

"Just hold up for a second, my nigga," Santos snapped back, trying to get him to calm down.

Santos's brain went into overdrive trying to come up with a quick plan. Since it was starting to get dark and the fact that they had gotten dinner, more than likely they were going to be there for the night. He was going to use that to his advantage as well. His only concern was Nyala and until she got out of harm's way, Santos was gonna move with caution.

Marco stood in the middle of his bedroom looking

up at the 72-inch TV on the wall. The news was on and the top story for the day was the shooting in Chinatown. He knew that it was Nikolai's work and he was kind of impressed.

As he stood there, he could hear the front door downstairs open and close. Marco had a few men downstairs so he knew that if there weren't any shots being fired, there wasn't a threat entering the house. He took another pull of his cigar and continued watching the news.

"You gotta be kidding me," Marco mumbled to himself as the news changed over to the weather report.

For some odd reason Marco could feel somebody staring at him and when he looked over, Nikolai was standing in the doorway. She stood there impeccably dressed, damn sure not looking like she just got finished doing everything Marco just saw on the news.

"I like your work," Marco commented, pointing his cigar at the TV. "I gotta keep my eyes on you." He smiled.

"You haven't seen nothing yet," Nikolai replied, entering the room.

She tossed her clutch onto his dresser and walked right up to Marco. She stood in front of him looking up at Marco with a seductive look in her eyes. Marco really didn't pay it any mind until he looked down at her.

"If you're scared, just tell me that you're scared," Nikolai said, inching closer to him.

All the shooting and killing made her horny as hell and all she wanted to do was fuck. It just so happened that Marco was the man of the hour.

"What are you talking about? Scared of what?" he said, taking another pull of his cigar.

"Me," she answered, stepping out of her heels.

Marco chuckled. He looked into her eyes and saw how serious she was, and then he noticed something about her that he never did before. He saw humbleness and submissiveness behind that toughness she'd been carrying around. That and the fact that Nikolai wasn't bad looking at all kind of turned Marco on.

"I'm not gonna be gentle," he said, taking another pull of his cigar and blowing the smoke in the air.

"I don't expect you to," she replied, inching closer.

He stuck to his word, reaching up and grabbing a handful of the back of her hair, yanking her head backwards and stuffing his tongue down her throat. She returned the favor giving him a mouth full of her tongue as well. His body towered over hers and for the first time in a long time Nikolai felt submissive.

With a fist full of her hair, he backed her up all the way to the wall, spun her around and slammed her body up against it. He rested the cigar in between his lips, reached down and hiked her skirt up over her waist all the while still clutching a fist full of her hair. It was rough and her face was planted into the wall, but she liked it. Having no panties gave Marco easy access and before his pants could hit the ground he was pushing his stiff meat inside of her from behind.

"Urrrgggggg," Nikolai grunted, as he pushed himself into her, up to his balls.

It wasn't the length, it was the girth that was killing her and Marco wasn't making it any easier to take as he pounded away at it. Marco lightly slamming her face up against the wall made Nikolai wetter which made it a little easier to deal with. After a while, her pussy got so slippery she was able to back her ass up and throw it on Marco.

"It don't hurt anymore," Nikolai looked back and told Marco as she spread both her ass cheeks apart so that he could go in deep.

He went in deeper and damn near busted. He quickly pulled out and spun her around to face him. She smiled, smacked his hand from off her hair and pushed him backwards onto the bed. She pulled her dress completely over her head, and then looked down at him.

"It's my turn now," she said, climbing on top of him with lust-filled eyes and a four-orgasm quota in mind.

Mitch pulled into the garage on the side of his condo's building and damn near ran into a crowd of men who were gathered around his parking space. He didn't know who it was so reaching for his gun was like second nature. It wasn't until he saw Ezra sitting on the trunk of one of his cars that he eased up on the trigger. Mitch still kept his gun in his hand as he got out of the car. Ezra had a drained look on his face giving Mitch the impression that Nikolai or Marco also attacked him. Mitch just didn't know the half.

"Ezra, wassup," Mitch said, extending his hand out for a shake.

Mitch counted at least 15 of Ezra's men, including the one at the entrance of the garage Mitch noticed when he came in and two more over by the double elevators. He still wasn't sure what type time Ezra was on, but until he found out the gun was going to stay in his hand, with the safety off.

"She killed my wife," Ezra spoke, surprising Mitch. "I need you to help me find this bitch so I can put a bullet in her head," Ezra said.

"Damn, Ezra. I'm sorry about your loss," Mitch said, finally tucking his gun away.

The crazy thing was that the whole way home Mitch was putting together a plan to get Nikolai and Marco to come out of hiding. He didn't know their location so he couldn't go to them; the only other way was to get them to come after him again, but this time be a little more prepared for when they showed up.

"Look, I might have a way to draw them out," Mitch said, looking around the room at some of Ezra's men. "I just can't guarantee nobody will be hurt," he said in a low voice so that Ezra's men wouldn't hear him.

Ezra didn't care about any collateral damage when it came down to it. Besides, his men were more than willing to die for him just as easy as it was for them to kill for him.

"Come on upstairs. I'll let you know what I got," Mitch told him, nodding for Ezra to follow.

Sosa raced down the highway at high speeds, dipping in and out of traffic. Trey had to tell her to slow down several times, but she paid him no mind. Her eyes were locked on the GPS and the road ahead of her, and her heart raced at the thought of losing Nyala again, this time maybe permanently if she didn't get to her fast enough.

Sosa's phone ringing snapped her out of the zone she was in. She wasn't going to answer it at first, but after she let it go to voicemail the first time, it started ringing again. She grabbed it from off the car charger and looked at the screen. It was Semaj.

"Wassup, Maj," Sosa answered, looking over at the GPS.

"They were here, but the motel manager said that they checked out early this morning," Semaj told her. "They should be in Florida by now."

"Yeah I'm here. I should be at the motel in about 20 minutes. I'll call you after I get there," Sosa said, looking in her rearview to make sure that it was safe for her to switch lanes.

"A'ight. Be careful, and Sosa... slow down!" Semaj said, knowing that more than likely Sosa would be speeding.

Sosa hung up the phone then looked over at Trey. "Let me get one," she said extending her hand out.

Trey had a license to carry and that's how he was legally able to fly in a private aircraft with his weapon on him. In this instance, he brought along a few handguns, so no matter where they landed everybody would be strapped, something that was a necessity.

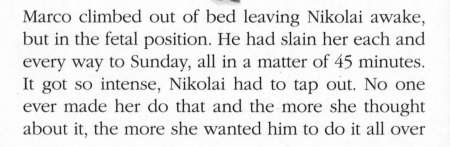

Marco climbed out of bed leaving Nikolai awake, but in the fetal position. He had slain her each and every way to Sunday, all in a matter of 45 minutes. It got so intense, Nikolai had to tap out. No one ever made her do that and the more she thought about it, the more she wanted him to do it all over again.

"Where are you going? It's late, come back to bed," Nikolai said, looking over at Marco as he was putting his pants back on.

"I gotta take care of something," Marco said, putting his shirt on. "You stay here and get your rest. It's gonna be a long day tomorrow and I need for you to be on your A game."

Nikolai rolled over onto her back, giggling and reaching down to rub her kitty. It turned her on to hear Marco sound like he was taking control of the situation. At this point, Marco was in so deep, he had no time to be bullshitting. He had to go all in and what better person to have by his side than Nikolai. She was rich, old enough to know better, but young enough to keep it sexy, brilliant, and her murder game was on 100. Marco didn't fear Nikolai, he simply respected her and after what just happened less than a half-hour ago, Marco would fuck around and wife her, if everything went as planned.

"Make the call," CJ spoke through clenched teeth, pointing the 9mm at the temple of the motel's clerk.

The young, white man picked up the phone without having to be asked a second time. Santos sat in the car with his seat all the way back, locked, loaded and waiting for his opportunity. He needed to move fast though because blood continued to leak from his wound and he was losing a lot of energy.

"Hello, this is the front desk," the clerk said, hearing Paulette pick up the phone. "I'm sorry to inform you, ma'am, but we have to switch your room," he told her, looking up at the gun that was pointed at his head.

"What do I need to change rooms for?" Paulette asked, grabbing the phone off the nightstand and walking over to the window. "We fine right here."

"Well, ma'am, the room you're in might have a leak. We just got a—"

"What kind of leak... oh hold on, I'll be right up," Paulette said, cutting him off.

She looked out of the window and scanned the parking lot for anything that resembled something suspicious. She wasn't taking any chances messing with Sosa and since Patrick was more than likely dead, there was no telling what he might have said before he died.

"Nyala, stay here and watch cartoons. I'll be right back," Paulette said, kneeling down in front of her.

"Okay, Aunt P," Nyala answered, looking at the TV screen.

Paulette got up and walked over to her black bag on the other end of the bed. She pulled out a 357 automatic, cocked a bullet in the chamber then stuffed it in the back of her waist. She also threw two extra clips into her pocket, just in case. She wasn't putting nothing past Sosa.

When she opened the door and stepped out of the room, she stood there and took another look around, scanning each and every car that was out there, along with rooms across the way. Nothing seemed to be out of place, so she proceeded to walk down the row towards the office.

"Change rooms my ass," she mumbled to herself, walking through the glass door and entering the small lobby area.

When Paulette looked over at the clerk, he slid out of his chair as though he was trying to get out of the way of something. That something was CJ, popping up from behind the counter with his gun pointed at Paulette. He squeezed. Pop! Pop! Pop!

One bullet hit her in the shoulder, spinning her around, the other two missed, shattering the glass door. As Paulette was falling to the ground, she pulled the .357 from her waist and let off two shots in CJ's direction. Neither one of them hit, but they forced him to take cover back behind the counter. It also gave her enough time to readjust herself, cup both hands around the gun for better aim, then wait for CJ to pop back up.

Santos heard the gun battle ensuing. He struggled getting out of the car and walking across the parking lot to the room Nyala was in. When he got to the door, it was locked, so he tapped on the window to get Nyala's attention. She got off the bed and walked over to the door thinking that it was Paulette.

"Come on, lift ya head up," Paulette whispered to herself.

Blood was leaking from her shoulder and she began to feel the pain of it. Her arms felt heavy and just when she was about to lower them, CJ popped up from behind the counter, aiming his gun. Paulette wasted no time in squeezing the trigger. Boom!

All CJ saw was the flash before the bullet broke through his front teeth and hit him in the back of his throat. She squeezed the trigger again, hitting him in his chest. He fell backward behind the counter.

"Nyala!" she yelled, rolling over onto her feet.

Paulette stumbled out the broken glass door and headed toward her room. She was about six doors down when Santos came out of her room holding Nyala's hand. Paulette raised her gun and so did Santos. Nyala hid behind Santos, scared out of her mind.

"Let her go!" Paulette yelled, inching closer.

"I can't do that," he replied, gripping his gun tighter.

It was a standoff and neither one of them

was budging. Both of them, however, were getting weaker from their wounds. Paulette was losing a lot of blood, but Santos had endured enough. His body couldn't take any more. It was as if everything went into slow motion. His legs became so weak, he buckled to his knees and he lowered his gun.

Paulette was about to shoot him, but decided against it because Nyala was still standing behind him. She lowered her gun, too, seeing how weak Santos looked. She walked over to grab Nyala so that they could leave, but as soon as she got within a few feet of Santos, he raised his gun up and began firing. Paulette saw it coming, but it was too late for her to do anything. Santos didn't just squeeze once, he kept pulling the trigger until he pumped ten hot lead balls into Paulette's body, knocking her backwards six steps before she collapsed in between two parked cars.

Santos popped the empty clip out and reached in his back pocket for his extra one. When he didn't feel it, he turned around, and standing there with the extra clip in her hand and passing it to him was Nyala. He looked at her and smiled; took the clip, slammed it into his gun, cocked one in the chamber, and scooped Nyala up as he stood to his feet.

He eased his way over to where Paulette had fallen, pointing his gun at her body in case she wasn't dead. Right as he walked up on her, a car turned into the parking lot at high speed. Santos didn't know who it was so he pointed the gun at the car. It came to a screeching halt, and then Santos heard a familiar voice yelling for Nyala. It was Sosa, getting out of the car and running towards them.

"Mommy! Mommy!" Nyala yelled, wiggling out of Santos's arms and running to her.

Sosa scooped her up and hugged her so tight, giving her kisses all over. Santos stood there looking on, happy that Nyala was safe with her mother again. His wound wouldn't allow for him to enjoy the reunion long. His legs gave out on him again and he buckled to his knees. Sosa put Nyala down and ran over to him.

"Get her in the car!" she yelled to Trey as she bent down next to Santos.

She could see that he was in bad shape. She threw his arm over her shoulder, helped him to his feet, then to the car. The sounds of sirens were in the distance, and right before the cops got to the scene, Sosa had pulled out of the parking lot with her family accounted for.

Chapter 19

"Thank goodness they got her," Semaj told Qua after hanging up the phone with Sosa. "She got Santos, too, and they're on their way to the airport right now."

"How the hell," Qua said, with confusion on his face. "I thought he was in New York."

Before Semaj could answer Qua, her phone began vibrating. She looked at the screen and didn't recognize the number, but answered it anyway.

"Semaj, this Ion, one of the men that work for your dad. I'm at the hospital with Vikingo and..." Ion hesitated. "I don't know how to tell you this, but Vikingo was murdered a couple of hours ago," he told her.

Semaj stood there in shock, letting the phone slip out of her hand and fall to the ground. Those words were worse than being shot. In fact, Semaj would have rather been shot then to have heard that her fiancé was killed.

"Yo, what up, Maj?" Qua asked, seeing the blank glare on her face.

She didn't have to answer him for Qua to know that Vikingo was dead. After all, it was him that gave the order for it to happen. Vikingo was the only thing that stood in between him and Semaj getting back together and he was at the point where he felt the need to kill all competition. He wanted Semaj back and he was going to get her back by any and all means necessary, even if that included her having to grieve for a couple of months behind Vikingo's death. At the end of the day, Qua knew that she would eventually find her way back to him and for the price of Vikingo's life, it was all worth it.

"Come on, ma. Let's get you home," Qua said, carefully escorting Semaj to the car for the long ride back to New York.

"Wheels are up in five minutes," the pilot announced when he boarded the jet.

Sosa sat in the chair directly across from Santos, watching him go in and out of consciousness. Trey walked up and passed Sosa a bottle of Ciroc with a cup. He knew she could use a drink.

"Is he gonna be alright?" Trey asked, looking over at the pale-faced Santos breathing lightly.

Sosa looked at Santos then over at Nyala asleep in the chair across the aisle. Hands down,

Santos was a beast. He survived a chest shot, left the hospital, and drove thousands of miles to Florida, only to get into another shoot-out in order to save a little girl that wasn't of any relation to him. Not only that, but he did it all with fragments of the bullet still lodged in his chest. He was tough as nails.

"Yeah, I think he's going to be alright," Sosa said with blind confidence.

Words couldn't explain how Sosa felt the moment she pulled into the motel's parking lot and saw Nyala in Santos's arms. He wasn't just Sosa's savior, he was her hero. For what he did, Sosa would always be grateful to him, and love him with the enormous amount of love no one has ever received from her. She felt that he earned that and more.

The long drive back to New York was quiet for the most part. Semaj didn't sleep at all. The only thing she did was stare aimlessly out of her window. She looked so distraught, it started to affect Qua. He hated seeing her look like this, especially for Vikingo, but he had to play it cool from here on out. Semaj thought that Nikolai was the one behind it and Qua wanted to keep it that way.

"Maj, I know this might not sound right coming from me, but I'm truly sorry for your loss,"

Qua said, breaking the silence in the car.

She looked over at Qua for a second then rolled her eyes right back out of the window. She didn't do that because she was mad, she just felt confused right now. Thinking about Vikingo had Semaj pondering over some other important things like her period being late. She didn't have any symptoms of being pregnant, but it was rare for her menstrual to be a day late, let alone seven.

"I'm late, Qua," Semaj said, as she continued staring out of the window.

"What you mean you 'late'?" Qua asked, looking over at her. "Maj!" he yelled, wanting her to answer him.

Semaj really didn't want to tell him and even now she couldn't figure out why she opened her mouth.

"Look, my period is a few days late," Semaj said, looking over at him.

"So, who you pregnant by?" he questioned with one eyebrow up.

"You, I haven't been with nobody else," she snapped, rolling her eyes. "Look, I know I started the conversation, but we're not gonna discuss this right now. I have to get back to the city and deal with my fiancé. So let's just leave it alone," Semaj said, and then turned back around to finish looking out the window.

Qua decided not to even pursue the conversation

any further. He could tell by her attitude that it would only turn into an argument. That was something he wanted to avoid. Anything that had the potential of pushing Semaj away from him would defeat the purpose of him doing what he did. Qua wasn't dumb by a long shot. He knew that all Semaj needed was time and space right now to grieve and he was going to give her just that.

Marco sat and watched as the three black trucks came out of Mitch's garage. The night sky provided a cover for him to be unnoticed and as the three trucks headed down, so did Marco.

"She's on the move," Marco spoke into his phone, tailing the caravan at a respected distance.

When Marco put in work, he made sure that he did it big and most of the time he hit his mark. He let Mitch get away back at Santos's house, but he wasn't about to make the same mistake twice. He was under the impression that Semaj was also in the truck, which was even better. Killing two birds with one stone was ideal, and if he could get it off, that's exactly what he was going to do.

"Make sure everybody dies," Marco said into the phone before hanging up.

Marco backed off from the truck, putting even more distance between them. It was for good reason. The three trucks stopped at a red light at

Broadway and Canal and the lead Tahoe became the target immediately. The driver didn't even see the man exiting his car from the corner of Canal Street. He looked like a regular pedestrian crossing the street on Broad and as he was passing in front of the first Tahoe, he came out of his jacket pocket with a grenade, pulled the pin and tossed it under the truck. The driver still didn't have a clue what he had done, and just as the light turned green and the truck began to pull off, the grenade went off, right under the gas tank. Boooooooooooom!

The blast lifted the truck several feet in the air, incinerating from the inside out. It landed back down on all four wheels, but was completely engulfed in flames. The blast rocked nearby cars and shattered a few business's front windows.

There had to be at least ten men who came from out of nowhere and began opening fire with large assault rifles at the other two trucks. Bullet after bullet ripped through the trucks, chipping through the bulletproof glass with ease. Neither one of the drivers were able to peel out since they were hit first.

As soon as the truck exploded, it seemed New York's finest were en route to the scene. One beat cop had walked up onto the mayhem, but eased off and walked the opposite way when he saw the kind of power the gunmen were using. He wasn't going to do anything until back up arrived.

"A'ight, that's my cue," Marco mumbled to himself, putting his car in reverse to back out of the street.

The headlight from an oncoming car blinded him as he turned to look out of the back window. Before he could turn around and put the car in drive, the oncoming vehicle had crashed right into him. The car hit him so hard, his airbags deployed and his car shut off.

"Got damn!" Marco yelled, pushing the airbag out of his face.

Murda Mitch and Ezra hopped out of the car that crashed into Marco's with guns in hand. The entire time Marco was following the trucks, Ezra and Mitch were following him. Mitch thought that if he drove around the city long enough, Marco or Nikolai would eventually bite the bait. Mitch was right.

Ezra walked up to the driver's side of Marco's car and fired a shot through the window. The bullet shattered the glass and hit Marco in the chest, but Ezra wasn't done with him. He opened the door and pulled Marco out of the car, throwing him to the ground then kneeling down over him.

"Where is she?" Ezra asked, looking into Marco's eyes.

"E, we gotta go," Mitch yelled, seeing red and blue lights flashing a couple of blocks away.

Marco looked up and laughed at Ezra. "She's

going to kill you. She's going to kill all of you."
Marco chuckled.

"Ezra!" Mitch yelled out again.

Knowing he was out of time, Ezra took his gun and shoved it into Marco's mouth, breaking some of his teeth off in the process. Marco's eyes widened and for the first time, Ezra could see the fear he'd been hiding all these years. He took pleasure in what he was about to do. Ezra pulled the trigger sending a bullet through the roof of Marco's mouth and into his brain. Out of hatred, he continued squeezing the trigger, sending multiple bullets through Marco's mouth and into his head. Mitch had to walk over and pull Ezra off of him as several police cars were coming down the street with their lights flashing. They drove right by Mitch and Ezra who faded into the night.

Ron was nervous as hell and had been all day, thinking about what he was going to do. It wasn't just jail time he was worried about, his life was literally on the line and he wanted to do everything in his power to preserve it, even if that meant sacrificing someone else's life instead. Him and Qua were like brothers and it ate at him knowing he put his best friend's life at risk, especially since Qua had been nothing, but loyal to him.

"Damn!" Ron huffed to himself, shaking his

head.

He looked down at his phone and pushed call, coming to the conclusion that this needed to be done. From here on out, there was no turning back for Ron and deep within his heart, he didn't want to anyway. This had been going on long enough and now it was time to bring it to an end.

"Davis, this is Ron. Meet me at the storage center tomorrow morning. You know, the one me and Qua met at before. Meet me on the west side of the lot, and bring a pair of lock cutters.

Chapter 20

Santos could hear people talking inside of the room, but his eyes felt so heavy, he was unable to open them right away. It took him a few minutes, but when he did finally open them, the first person he saw was Nyala, sitting in a chair looking up at the TV. He knew from a quick glance around the room that he was in a hospital. He tried to say Nyala's name, but his throat was so dry it prevented him from doing so. He had to pluck the metal tail on the side of his bed to get her attention.

When Nyala looked over and saw Santos's eyes opened, she jumped out of her chair and ran over to his bedside. "Mommy! Mommy!" she yelled out, jumping up and down with a huge smile on her face.

Sosa came out of the bathroom and was about to tell Nyala to keep it down, but when she saw her standing by his bed, she knew that Santos must have woken up.

"Hey, sleepy head." Sosa smiled.

"Hi, Santos," Nyala playfully greeted. "Don't go back to sleep," she said, making funny faces at him.

"Yeah, because you almost died on us, boy, three times," Sosa said, sticking three fingers up. "Don't ever do that again, I swear I can't afford to lose you."

Santos tried to find some type of spit to wet his mouth so that he could talk, but none was there. He wanted to tell her how much he loved her, but from the look he had in his eyes, he didn't have to say a word.

"Thank you," Sosa said softly, grabbing his hand gently. "I love you so much, and I don't ever want to be without you," she told him as her eyes began to water over.

Santos cracked a smile then squeezed her hand. He loved her, too, and it was proven by his actions even before he did what he did. Putting his life on the line to save Nyala was only the icing on the cake. The way Sosa felt about him now, was even deeper.

"I was thinking, maybe after you get better..." she said, reaching into her jacket pocket. "I was wondering if you would consider being my husband?" Sosa pulled out a small black box.

She opened it revealing a platinum male wedding band with diamonds engraved in it. Santos looked at the ring and then back up at her with a serious look on his face. It kind of confused Sosa for a second, but then he smiled and squeezed her hand. The tears that filled up in Sosa's eyes began to fall, and this was the first time in her life she cried out of happiness. This was the first time she ever loved a man as much as she loved Santos.

It was sad to say, but Semaj didn't even have time to begin the mourning process for Vikingo. She had so much going on in her life right now, and to stop and do that would only make her vulnerable, something that she couldn't afford to be right now with Nikolai still out there.

"What room are they in?" Semaj wanted to know as she exited the coroner's room where she saw Vikingo's body for the very first time since being back in New York.

Her five-inch heels clicked through the hallways of the hospital as she made her way up to Santos's room. She had changed into a pair of cream slacks, a white blouse and a cream blazer making her hospital friendly and also very boss-like. Murda Mitch and Qua walking behind her only enhanced her look.

As soon as she got to the room, Nyala ran into her arms, happy to see her. Sosa had made her way onto the bed with Santos, curled up as much as she could be without hurting him. Semaj heard about his work and respected the hell out of Santos for going so hard for her niece.

"Thank you," Semaj said, walking over and kissing him on his forehead. Semaj quickly turned her attention over to Sosa. "We need to talk," she said, nodding towards the door.

Sosa knew that it was important so she eased up out of the bed, but not before kissing Santos. As they were leaving the room, Semaj stopped at the door and turned around to see where Nyala was. She was still sitting on the chair next to Santos's bed. Semaj looked at Sosa and wondered if she was going to bring her along. Sosa looked at Nyala then at Santos and smiled.

"She's safe here with him," Sosa said with confidence, then left the room, closing the door behind her.

"Come on my nigga, pick up," Ron said with his phone to his ear and his hand on the steering wheel.

He had been trying to call Qua for the past 25 minutes, hoping that he would pick up. Qua wasn't going to at first, but Ron kept on calling and calling and calling. He simply wore Qua down.

"Yo, what up," Qua answered, walking behind Semaj and Sosa down the hallway. "I thought I told you—"

"I know brah, but I need you. I told you I was going to fix this shit and today's the day, my nigga," Ron said.

"Yeah is that right?" Qua responded, unenthused by what Ron was talking about.

"Listen, brah. I need you to meet me at that storage joint—park on the east side of the lot. You should be able to see my car on the other end," Ron instructed.

"What's suppose to happen if I come?"

"Look, I told you, I'ma make dis' shit right," Ron told him. "I gotta go, brah. Please show up," Ron said before hanging up the phone.

Nikolai walked from the bedroom, to the main bathroom down the hall in Marco's bathrobe. When she got there she unraveled the straps and let the robe drop to the ground before walking over to the oval shaped bathtub in the middle of the floor. Aside from the hot bubble bath she prepared for herself, the bathroom provided her with a beautiful view of the wilderness that rested in Marco's own backyard. It was peaceful and for the moment, Nikolai wanted to enjoy it not knowing that darkness was right around the corner.

It took Ron every bit of an hour to get back to the

borough. When he pulled into the storage facility, the first thing he looked for was Qua's car. It wasn't there, but that wasn't going to stop him from doing what he had to do.

On the west side, where he was supposed to meet Davis and Mason, they were sitting in their car, waiting. Ron pulled in right behind them and turned his car off. Even at this point, Ron was nervous as hell and scared to death about the outcome to what he was about to do. He looked down the other end of the storage lot to see if Qua had showed up yet, but he hadn't. He was all alone.

"Go hard or go home," Ron mumbled to himself as he approached the passenger side of their car. Mason rolled his window down to talk.

"Whacha got for us, Ron?" Mason asked, looking over at the storage units lined up down the row.

"You got all that shit I asked you for?" Ron shot back.

"What da hell does that look like," Davis replied, pointing to the back seat with his thumb. "Now, tell me whacha got or you might as well jump in da fuckin' back seat with it," Davis threatened.

"Look, mafucka, I got five hundred kilos for you, and a shit load of guns. I just wanna make sure you got my shit right," Ron barked.

Five hundred kilos and some guns sounded like music to Davis's ears. It kind of made him forget all about the way Ron snapped on him. "Yeah, man. All of your shit is back there," Davis said in a calmer tone. "Now, which storage unit is the shit in?"

"Let me get this straight," Ron began. "So everything you took out of my car is right there?"

"Yes," Mason answered.

"And we're the only ones who know about all this?" Ron said, looking around. "We're the only ones who know about Qua, these drugs, Sosa, and everything I told you," Ron verified.

"Yeah, Ron, just us," Mason assured him.

That's all Ron needed to know. He reached into his back waist and pulled out a black .45 Millennium, pointed it at Mason's head and pulled the trigger. The bullet ripped through his skull killing him instantly. He pointed it at Davis, but Davis rolled out of the car, though not before Ron shot him twice. One bullet hit Davis on his right buttocks and the other hit him on the top of his back by his right shoulder.

By the time Davis turned, spun around, and drew his weapon, Ron had jumped on the front hood of the car and had his gun pointed at him. Davis had his gun pointed at Ron, too, and they both stood there staring at each other.

"Don't do this, Ron!" Davis shouted, gripping his gun tighter. "You don't wanna die like this."

Davis could see that his words didn't mean

anything to Ron, who looked down on him with fearless eyes. As Ron began pulling the trigger so did Agent Davis.

Pow! Pow! Pop! Pop! Pow! Pow! Pop! Pow! Pop! Pow!

They both stood there shooting at each other at close range and at high speeds. Pure adrenaline was what powered them to stand there and take as many bullets as they did from each other. It was the fatal headshot Ron took that ended the three-second-gun battle. The bullet hit Ron on the left side of his forehead knocking him backwards off the car.

It was as if Davis had become weak instantly. He looked down at his shirt and saw that it went from the color white, to the color red all over. He dropped down to his knees, then tried to retrieve his cell phone from his pant's pocket to call for help, but the phone never made it out of his pocket. From his knees, Davis fell flat on his face and died within a couple of minutes of lying there. All three men died, but only one died for a cause and that was Ron.

Qua and Semaj were in Qua's BMW, Sosa drove her Aston Martin and Murda Mitch was in a white Audi A-8. Semaj hadn't been up in Albany in a long time so her directions to Marco's house took a little longer than the actual time. Nevertheless, all three cars pulled up to Marco's house by noon. They jumped out of their cars and looked around at the quiet, rural area. Semaj looked up at Marco's house and noticed the strangest thing. Nikolai was sitting out on the master bedroom's balcony, looking down on all of them.

"We gon' go around back," Qua said about him and Mitch. "Y'all two stay here until we get back."

"Nah, nah, nah, just hold up for a second. Look," Semaj told them as she pointed at Nikolai sitting up there. "Let me check something out real quick," she said, easing away from them.

"Aye, Semaj. What da fuck is you doin'?" Qua snapped, walking towards her. "If you don't get yo' ass over here…" he demanded in a serious tone.

The first thing that came to his mind was the baby, and he'd be damned if she went in there by herself. Semaj pulled a spin move on him and told him that she wasn't going anywhere, but on the walkway. Qua was reluctant, but her let her go. She walked up the walkway and stopped by the balcony where she was able to look up and hear Nikolai.

"Are you here by yourself?" Semaj asked, looking up at Nikolai sipping from a clear glass.

Nikolai replied with a simple nod of the head. "So, how do you wanna do this?" Semaj asked her as she put her hair in a ponytail.

For Nikolai, this beef with Semaj had become personal. There was a lot more at stake pertaining to this ongoing war, but Nikolai had only one thing on her mind and that was to personally put a bullet in Semaj's head. That's all she lived for right now and she would risk everything, even her own life to see that through.

"Just me and you," Nikolai said, taking another sip of the scotch in her glass. "Woman to woman," Nikolai calmly suggested.

Semaj looked back at her people standing there, waiting for the green light to move. Semaj didn't want them to move out for her though. This beef had become personal for her, too, and she wanted to be the person that killed Nikolai. The offer of a one on one was starting to sound better by the minute.

"Just me and you, right?"

"Yup, just me and you," Nikolai replied, throwing back the last of her drink.

Semaj turned around and looked at her people again. "STAY HERE! I'LL BE RIGHT BACK!" Semaj yelled out.

Qua started to go in behind her, but Mitch grabbed him by the arm. He knew what was going down off the break and if Semaj wanted to handle this alone, Mitch was going to let her; win, lose, or draw.

"Let my princess be a woman," Mitch told

Qua with a stern look on his face. "Aye, you too." He looked over and told Sosa who seemed like she was inching away towards the house.

Semaj continued up the walk towards the entrance. Seeing Semaj walk through the door, she got up from her seat, looked out to Murda Mitch and smiled before fading away into the bedroom. Qua sucked his teeth and put his hands in the air. Mitch just stayed cool.

Once inside of the house, Semaj came out of her pumps and placed them neatly by the door. She then unbuttoned her blazer, reached in and pulled out a 17 shot Glock 9mm with a mini scope on it. There was no need to make sure a bullet was in the chamber because she did all that in the car before she got there. Semaj stayed on point.

She eased her way further into the house, listening and watching out for any movement. Both of her hands were wrapped around the gun and she had it extended in front of her like she'd trained for S.W.A.T.

"You know, I never liked you," the voice of Nikolai echoed throughout the house. "I never liked your grandmother, either," Nikolai continued.

Semaj could hear her but she couldn't see her and as Semaj continued to make her way through the downstairs of the house, the voice continued.

"I'm not afraid of you, Semaj."

"Yeah, well why don't you come out from

wherever you're hiding and say it to my face."

Semaj looked around as she headed towards the long spiral steps that led upstairs. Her foot only cleared one step when Nikolai came to the top of the steps holding a 223 assault rifle in her hands. With this sort of gun, Nikolai really didn't need aim. Doom! Doom! Doom! Doom! Doom! Doom! Doom! Doom! Doom! Doom!

Nikolai let it go, forcing Semaj to duck behind the wall that separated the living room from the dining room. Mitch, Qua, and Sosa heard the loud shots from outside and raced to the front door of the house. Qua opened the front door and the first thing he saw was Semaj squatting down with her gun in her hand and her back up against the wall.

She put her hand up to stop them in their tracks at the door. Shaking her head no, she waved for them to go back outside. It may have looked like she was at a disadvantage, but in her eyes she wasn't. The 223 rifle was huge and difficult to maneuver, as opposed to someone who was like a surgeon with a handgun. Semaj wanted to expose that.

"Maj!" Qua whispered, loud enough so she could hear him.

"Go!" she shot back, waving him off.

Qua reluctantly backed away from the door, but not before sliding his Glock across the floor to her.

"Come out, come out, wherever you are!"

Nikolai yelled out, easing her way down the steps.

Semaj did need to get herself in a better position to get the shot off that she wanted. The only thing that stood in between her and Nikolai was a wall made from a thin piece of wood. The 223 shells would slice right through it with ease.

Semaj stood up, gripped both guns in her hands and took in a deep breath. In a flash, she took off across the room, heading for the kitchen where there were more things to take cover around. It would also put her in a better position to get a good shot off.

Doom! Doom! Doom! Doom! Doom! Doom! Doom!

Nikolai tried to chase her down with the large rifle. Bullets tore up the ground behind every step Semaj ran.

Pop! Pop! Pop! Pop! Pop! Pop! Pop! Pop!

Semaj returned fire with both guns as she darted across the room. One of the bullets hit Nikolai in her thigh. She stumbled down a couple of steps but regained her balance. The cost of it was her having to drop the rifle and grab her leg. The .223 rifle tumbled down the steps until it hit the bottom. Semaj was trying to get out of the way of those bullets that she didn't even notice what had happened. She just got to the kitchen and dove behind the large island.

Nikolai scurried down the steps to retrieve

the gun, but when she got to it, Semaj popped up from behind the island. Semaj dropped Qua's Glock then cupped both of her hands around her gun. She had Nikolai's full body in the eye of her scope and when Nikolai bent over to retrieve the .223 rifle, Semaj closed one eye, took in a deep breath and squeezed. Pop! Pop! Pop!

Semaj sent three bullets in Nikolai's direction, hitting her twice, once in her side and the other in Nikolai's arm. The impact from the bullet to her side knocked Nikolai up against the wall. From the wall, Nikolai slid to the ground and still tried to reach for the rifle, but her wounds made it hard for her to extend her reach.

Semaj slowly walked over to Nikolai, lowering her gun after seeing that Nikolai was pretty much finished. When she got up close on her, Semaj tucked her gun into her back pocket, reached down and picked up the assault rifle. The theme music from the movie *Scarface*, when Tony shot Manny in the doorway, sounded off in Semaj's head. She looked at the large rifle then looked down at Nikolai. This was the moment she had been waiting for far too long. This was for all the attempts made on Semaj's life, all the innocent people that were killed as a result of those attempts. This was for all the time and money wasted behind Nikolai's foolishness, and for the disrespect, lack of loyalty and ungratefulness to the 16 Tent. It was time for retribution.

"Tell Satan I couldn't make it," Semaj said, raising the large rifle and pointing it at Nikolai's face.

Semaj squeezed the trigger and held it. Doom! Doom! Doom! Doom! Doom! Doom! The bullets tore through Nikolai's face, knocking chunks of flesh and bones all over the wall behind her. To see it happen and be the one who was doing it, Semaj felt the instant gratification she'd been yearning for far too long. Words couldn't express how she felt inside, but one thing she did know, looking down at the remains of Nikolai's body, it was all over. The threat was finally neutralized and the war was over. No more running around fearing for her life, and no more putting her life on hold. This was it. This was the end. Semaj Monique Richardson Espriella is truly the only real Mafia Princess.

Nine Months Later

"Push, babe," Qua said as Samaj used the breathing technique the doctor taught her.

Instead of having her baby in the hospital, Semaj decided to deliver her child in the comfort of her own home in Colombia. The feeling of being surrounded by family during these times would have been overwhelming.

"Come on, give me one more big push," the doctor said, cupping his hands around the tip of the baby's head.

Semaj took in a deep breath and pushed as hard as she could, praying that this would be her final attempt. She had been in labor for over five hours and it was kicking her ass. As Semaj pushed, Qua held her hand tight, then moments later, a caramel, bloody, bushy haired baby girl made her way into the world. Semaj and Qua had already named her Marissa.

Being the father, Qua was afforded the

opportunity to cut the umbilical cord along with washing the baby off. The baby's cries brought tears to his eyes. After counting ten fingers and ten toes, he brought baby Marissa over to Semaj. Qua had to be the happiest man alive right now.

"Thank you," he whispered into Semaj's ear, and then kissed her on the side of her head.

God had finally blessed him with what he'd been asking for since the day he met Semaj. God had blessed him with the greatest gift a man could ask for, and that was the blessing of a family.

Murda Mitch, Sosa, Ezra, Lu Wang, Bashir Amad, Selina, and Dameon Fashkon sat at the brown, marble, round table talking amongst themselves quietly, waiting for Semaj to join them. The other good thing about Semaj giving birth at home was the fact that everything she needed for a speedy recovery was right there. It had been less than forty-eight hours since she delivered her baby and she was already back to business, attending a meeting that was previously arranged. She was fortunate that the meeting was at her house, which made it even easier for her to make it.

Semaj was still a little weak, but she managed to walk down the steps from her bedroom to the conference room in the south wing of her home, all by herself. The moment she stepped foot into the room it became quiet and all eyes were on her.

"I called this meeting today so that I may introduce the new members of the 16 Tent," Semaj said, taking a seat at the table.

Lu Wang was from South Korea, but grew up in Cambodia and controlled 70% of heroin production. She was very educated and was able to read, write, speak and understand twelve different languages fluently. Her ability to hold firm in the jungles against hundreds of domestic gorillas, showed that she wasn't a pushover and could go as hard as the best of them.

Bashir Amad resided in Yemen. He wasn't a drug dealer nor was he a gunrunner. Bashir was an oil driller, and he stored millions and millions of gallons of oil and sold it on the black market for prices the American government would kill for.

Dameon Fashkon didn't just sell guns, he made them and produced some of the most advanced handguns and assault rifles known to man. He was so vicious, the Russian government in Moscow didn't want to touch him. They feared him, but at the same time they needed his technology for future wars. He was considered to be the untouched marksman and earned every bit of his status.

Sosa, Ezra, Mitch, and Selina all reclaimed their original places at the table. Mitch continued to hold it down in London while Selina stepped all the way up for Cuba. As far as Sosa, who recently got married to Santos and was four months pregnant, she kept her foot on the neck of New York. With Qua and Semaj now being married and living in Colombia, the city of New York was all hers, completely.

"I'm moving the 16 Tent into a new direction," Semaj spoke. "We will no longer be divided amongst each other nor will we be governed by some of the old rules of the past," she said, looking around the room. "This is a family, our family, and just like every family, there is a leader. I am the head of this family and if anybody has any objections to what I just said, please feel free to get up and leave."

No one moved. Everybody sat there accepting the position Semaj just took. Most felt like she had earned her position while the new members were simply honored to be sitting at the table with her. And just like that, the 16 Tent was rebuilt with a brighter future ahead, and a leader that would give her life to see that this family would never part. Semaj was no longer the Mafia Princess; she was now the Tent's Queen.

The End

Prologue

"Push! Push!" the doctor directed Kim, as he held the top of the baby's head, hoping this would be the final push that would bring a new life into the world.

The hospital's delivery room was packed with both Kim and Drake's family, and although the large crowd irritated Drake, he still managed to video record the birth of his son. After four hours of labor, Kim gave birth to a 6.5-pound baby boy, who they already named Derrick Jamal Henson Jr. Drake couldn't help but to shed a few tears of joy at the new addition to his family, but the harsh reality of his son's safety quickly replaced his joy with anger.

Drake was nobody's angel and beyond his light brown eyes and charming smile, he was one of the most feared men in the city of Philadelphia, due to his street cred. He put a lot of work in on the blocks of South Philly, where he grew up. He mainly pushed drugs and gambled, but from time to time he'd place well-known dealers into the trunk of his car and hold them for ransom, according to how much that person was worth.

"I need everybody to leave the room for awhile," Drake told the people in the hospital room, wanting to share a private moment alone with Kim and his son.

The families took a few minutes saying their goodbyes, before leaving. Kim and Drake sat alone in the room, rejoicing over the birth of baby Derrick. The only interruption was doctors coming in and out of the room to check up on the baby, mainly because they were a little concerned about his breathing. The doctor informed Drake that he would run a few more tests to make sure the baby would be fine.

"So, what are you going to do?" Kim questioned Drake, while he was cradling the baby.

"Do about what?" he shot back, without lifting his head up. Drake knew what Kim was alluding to, but he had no interest in discussing it. Once Kim became pregnant, Drake agreed to leave the street life alone, if not completely then significantly cutting back after their baby was born. They both feared if he didn't stop living that street life, he would land in the box. Drake felt he and jail were like night and day: they could never be together.

"You know what I'm talking about, Drake. Don't play stupid with me," Kim said, poking him in his head with her forefinger.

He smiled. "I gave you my word I was out of the game when you had our baby. Unless my eyes are deceiving me, I think what I'm holding in my arms is our son. Just give me a couple of days to clean up the streets and then we can sit down and come up with a plan on how to invest the money we got."

Cleaning up the streets meant selling all the drugs he had and collecting the paper owed to him from his workers and guys he fronted weight to. All together, there was about 100-k due, not to mention the fact he had to appoint someone to take over his bread-winning crack houses and street corners that made him millions of dollars.

Drake's thoughts came to a halt when his phone started to ring. Sending the call straight to voicemail didn't help any because it rang again. Right when he reached to turn the phone off, he noticed it was Peaches calling. If it were anybody else, he probably would've declined, but Peaches wasn't just anybody.

"Yo," he answered, shifting the baby to his other arm while

trying to avoid Kim's eyes cutting over at him.

"He knows! He knows everything!" Peaches yelled, with terror in her voice.

Peaches wasn't getting good reception out in the woods where Villain had left her for dead, so the words Drake was hearing were broken up. All he understood was, "Villain knows!" That was enough to get his heart racing. His heart wasn't racing out of fear, but rather excitement.

In many ways, Villain and Drake were cut from the same cloth. They even both shared tattoos of several teardrops under their eyes. It seemed like gunplay was the only thing that turned Drake on—besides fucking—and when he could feel it in the air, murder was the only thing on his mind.

Drake hung up the phone and tried to call Peaches back to see if he could get better reception, but her phone went straight to voicemail. Damn! he thought to himself as he tried to call her back repeatedly and block out Kim's voice as she steadily asked him if everything was alright.

"Drake, what's wrong?"

"Nothing. I gotta go. I'll be back in a couple of hours," he said, handing Kim their son.

"How sweet! There's nothing like family!" said a voice coming from the direction of the door.

Not yet lifting his head up from his son to see who had entered the room, at first Drake thought it was a doctor, but once the sound of the familiar voice kicked in, Drake's heart began beating at an even more rapid pace. He turned to see Villain standing in the doorway, chewing on a straw and clutching what appeared to be a gun at his waist. Drake's first instinct was to reach for his own weapon, but remembering that he left it in the car made his insides burn. Surely, if he had his gun on him, there would have been a showdown right there in the hospital.

"Can I come in?" Villain asked in an arrogant tone, as he made his way over to the visitors' chairs. "Let me start off by saying congratulations on having a bastard child."

Villain's remarks made Drake's jaw flutter continuously from fury. Sensing shit was about to go left, Kim attempted to get out of the bed with her baby to leave the room, but before her feet could hit the floor, Villain pulled out a .50 Caliber Desert Eagle and placed it on his lap. The gun was so enormous that Drake could damn near read off the serial number on the slide. Kim looked at the nurse's button and was tempted to press it.

"Push the button and I'll kill all three of y'all. Scream, and I'ma kill all three of y'all. Bitch," Villian paused, making sure the words sunk in, "if you even blink the wrong way, I'ma kill all three of y'all."

"What the fuck you want?" Drake asked, still trying to be firm in his speech.

"You know, at first, I thought about getting my money back and then killin' you for setting my brother up wit' those bitches you got working for you. But on my way here I just said, 'Fuck the money!' I just wanna kill the nigga."

Deep down inside, Drake wanted to ask for his life to be spared, but his pride wouldn't allow it. Not even the fact that his newborn son was in the room could make Drake beg to stay alive, which made Villain more eager to lullaby his ass into a permanent sleep.

Villain wanted to see the fear in his eyes before he pulled the trigger, but Drake was a G, and was bound to play that role 'til he kissed death.

"Flyer Than A Piece Of Paper Bearin' My Name/ Got The Hottest Chick In The Game Wearin' My Chain..."

Aaliyah

"Mommy... Mommy... wake up! Pleaaaase, Mommy, wake up! You can't die. Dear God, I beg you, please, don't let my mother die!" During the ride in the ambulance, those words I pleaded to God, as I watched my dad hold my mother's lifeless body in his arms, kept replaying in my head. I seemed to be trapped in somebody else's nightmare, but the more I witnessed the paramedic and emergency medical technician doing everything they could to keep my mother alive, the more I had to accept this nightmare was my reality.

"Daddy, she can't die... not like this," my voice trailed off as I held on to my father's hand tightly, hoping it would somehow bring me strength.

"I've done this before. When does it stop? I guess never." When my father said those words, it took a minute for them to sink in.

"What do you mean you've done this before?"

"Your mother almost died in my arms years ago. Before you were born. She was shot, just like she was today, and lost our baby. That was the worst day of my life and now this is the second."

This was the first time I heard anything about this. Before I could ask my father to further elaborate, we had arrived at the hospital. In an instant, the pace went into overdrive. They rushed my mother into surgery and all we could do was pray. I grabbed onto my dad's arm and held it tightly.

"Please, move aside," a male voice barked at us.

"Omigoodness, that's Genesis." And then I noticed my dad. "Daddy!" I yelled out when I saw them being brought in on stretchers. Right behind them was Amir. "Amir, what happened? Is it bad?"

I was so caught up with what happened to my mother, I had no idea Genesis and my dad had also been hurt. I prayed they weren't on the brink of death, like my mother. This nightmare was getting worse and worse with each second.

"They've both been shot, but the injuries aren't life-threatening. It's not bad," Amir explained.

"Thank goodness. There's only so much more of this I can take."

"How's your mom?"

"Not good," I said, putting my head down, now wanting the tears to start pouring all over again.

"Aaliyah, I'm sorry," Amir said, holding me closely.

"I don't know what I'll do if she doesn't make it."

"I got here as soon as I heard. How's Precious?" I looked up and saw Lorenzo standing in front of us. Instead of answering Lorenzo's question, I continued to cry.

"It's not looking good," Amir said, answering for me.

"No, not Precious," Lorenzo kept repeating, with his voice breaking up. He put his hands up and repeatedly shook his head, as if in denial. He then walked off and I saw him talking to a triage nurse. I guess Lorenzo was searching for the same answers we all wanted.

Amir and I went to sit down next to my dad. We all remained silent, as if scared to speak. This went on for what felt like forever and the silence made me feel like my head was going to explode.

"Aaliyah, do you want anything? I'ma go get something to drink."

"I'll take anything with caffeine, since I'll be up all night."

"What about you, Supreme. Can I get you something?"

"I'm Dad."

"Dad, you sure you don't want anything?"

"Yes," he said, and walked off. I knew my mother's condition was eating him up; hell, I was barely keeping it together, but I hated seeing him so broken up. So many thoughts were going through my head and as I began to get lost in them, from a distance I noticed Lorenzo. I decided to go speak to him and see if the triage nurse had told him anything we didn't already know. I seriously doubted it, but I was grasping for any sign of optimism at this point.

As I got closer, I realized Lorenzo was on the phone. He was in a deep conversation. I decided to get close enough where I could hear what he was saying, but without him noticing me.

"Dior, I can't come to LA right now. Someone very close to me is in the hospital. Yes, it's a woman. Why are you asking me that?"

Damn, I wish I could hear what this Dior chick is saying, I thought to myself.

"Yes, I love her." There was a long pause before Lorenzo continued, "And I do love you, too," he said, in an almost frustrated tone. "I don't want to get into a discussion about my feelings for you or Precious, right now. I have to go. I'll talk to you tomorrow."

When Lorenzo got off the phone he turned around and I could see the surprise on his face when he saw me. "Aaliyah, I didn't realize you were standing over here."

"I'm sure you didn't, being that you were so deep into your conversation," I said sarcastically.

"I'm assuming you were listening."

"Of course I was. You claim to care so much about my mother, but you were on the phone with some chick named Dior. You are such the quintessential player."

"It's not like that, Aaliyah."

"So says the man that's on the phone proclaiming his love

to another woman, while my mother is fighting for her life."

"Your mother knows all about Dior. She was a woman I was engaged to before I ever met Precious. I thought she was dead. During my relationship with your mother, I found out Dior was alive. That's why Precious broke things off with me, but I never stopped loving her. Honestly, when I heard that she might die, I realized how in love with her I am. I want to be right by your mother's side when she wakes up."

"So, you think she's gonna make it?"

"I have to believe that and so do you. I can't consider anything else. Aaliyah, I know you never really cared for me."

"It's not that. It's just that…"

"You blamed me for breaking up your mother and father," Lorenzo said, finishing my thought.

"I did blame you initially, but like I told you before, I realized their marriage was already over before you came into her life. I will admit, I always wanted them back together and felt you were in the way."

"I get that. Please know your mother is very important to me. After Dior, I didn't believe I could ever fall in love with another woman again. Precious proved me wrong."

"She has that effect on men." I smiled. "I do believe you love her, Lorenzo, and I'm glad you're here. My mother needs everyone's support right now, including yours."

I glanced over at my dad and then back at Lorenzo. Both men loved her and so many other people did, too, but none more than me. If my mother didn't survive, all of our lives would change and nothing would ever be the same again.

Order Form

A King Production
P.O. Box 912
Collierville, TN 38027
www.joydejaking.com
www.twitter.com/joydejaking

Name: _____
Address: _____
City/State: _____
Zip: _____

QUANTITY	TITLES	PRICE	TOTAL
_____	Bitch	$15.00	_____
_____	Bitch Reloaded	$15.00	_____
_____	The Bitch Is Back	$15.00	_____
_____	Queen Bitch	$15.00	_____
_____	Last Bitch Standing	$15.00	_____
_____	Superstar	$15.00	_____
_____	Ride Wit' Me	$12.00	_____
_____	Stackin' Paper	$15.00	_____
_____	Trife Life To Lavish	$15.00	_____
_____	Trife Life To Lavish II	$15.00	_____
_____	Stackin' Paper II	$15.00	_____
_____	Rich or Famous	$15.00	_____
_____	Rich or Famous Part 2	$15.00	_____
_____	Bitch A New Beginning	$15.00	_____
_____	Mafia Princess Part 1	$15.00	_____
_____	Mafia Princess Part 2	$15.00	_____
_____	Mafia Princess Part 3	$15.00	_____
_____	Mafia Princess Part 4	$15.00	_____
_____	Boss Bitch	$15.00	_____
_____	Baller Bitches Vol. 1	$15.00	_____
_____	Baller Bitches Vol. 2	$15.00	_____
_____	Bad Bitch	$15.00	_____
_____	Still The Baddest Bitch	$15.00	_____
_____	Power	$15.00	_____
_____	Power 2	$15.00	_____
_____	Princess Fever "Birthday Bash"	$9.99	_____

Shipping/Handling (Via Priority Mail) $6.50 1-2 Books, $8.95 3-4 Books add $1.95 for ea. Additional book.

Total: $_____ FORMS OF ACCEPTED PAYMENTS: Certified or government issued checks and money Orders, all mail in orders take 5-7 Business days to be delivered